CRÈME BRÛLÉE TO SLAY

CEECEE JAMES

For my Family

CONTENTS

BLURB

Georgie Tanner's excitement to be part of her historic town's annual Franco-American commemorative charity event, but fun turns to tragedy when Gainesville's least favorite resident drops dead at the party. In the chaos that follows the town harpy's death, a priceless heirloom goes missing—the sword George Washington gave to the war hero who detained Benedict Arnold.

While Georgie is always ready to help her town solve a mystery, this one turns personal when someone suspects that Georgie may have been the one to serve the toxic dish! She must identify the culprit before she becomes the primary suspect... although as the investigation progresses, it's not long before being a murder suspect is the least of her worries.

CHAPTER 1

*S*ome mornings start out great. Some are more of a *three cups of coffee before you talk to me* kind of day. But this morning began with someone saying they wanted to kill me.

Granted, that person was Kari Missler, my best friend of thirteen years. Though her threat was half-hearted, there was a tone in her voice that made me wonder exactly where our friendship stood at the moment.

"Georgie Tanner," her voice growled on the other end of the cell phone. "I've just been cornered by Mrs. Vanderton for *ten minutes* at the grocery store, her finger shaking and everything, yelling at me about what a terrible person I was. You know how she is—picture her screeching at you, with her dyed black hair in those ridiculous fat curls just quivering with indignation. I had to stand there, juggling milk and fruit, while she went on and on. Luckily Colby took off, so I had an excuse to go. Otherwise, I'd probably still be trapped there. And it's all your fault."

Colby was Kari's nine-year-old son, and very active and always on the brink of trouble. She had more than one hair-raising story of rescuing that boy. It's probably how, even after having two kids, she was still the same size as when she was a teenager in high school.

I was about to ask how it was my fault when Kari rattled on. "I was there for you when you volunteered me for the zoo parental supervisor for the day care. I was there when you volunteered me for the town's clean-up day. But this ... this is too much. You made me look like such a jerk." She huffed a sigh, and I could almost see her roll her eyes.

Thoroughly confused, I blurted out, "What did I do?"

"The charity dinner! We're going, and you're the one serving us!"

Ah, I understood. The charity dinner Kari was referring too was an annual event that Mr. and Mrs. Miquel held in commemoration of the moment when George Washington awarded John Paulding a ceremonial sword and the Fidelity Medallion, the first military decoration ever given. He'd earned the award for capturing British Major John Andre, the spy who tried to set Benedict Arnold free through his surrender to the British. The crowning moment of the event was the display of the actual sword. The money donated went to Gainesville parks and museums for the upkeep of the American Revolution memorabilia. Mr. Miquel was very proud of the sword and his event, and only those with very deep pockets were invited to attend.

So there I am," Kari continued grousing, "clutching my blueberries in one hand, and trying to get Colby out of the soda display, while attempting to figure out why Mrs. Vanderton is so angry. Apparently, she thinks it's very priggish of me to attend the dinner with you serving. I was so shocked that you didn't tell me you'd be there that I didn't know what to say. She has *such* a way of making you feel like a jerk. I wished I'd told her to mind her own business. But it does bring up a good point. How *am* I'm supposed to enjoy myself sitting all posh while you're working to make us happy? I don't understand why would you do something like that on Valentine's Day? The dinner always has plenty of help."

"I'm sorry you got yelled at on behalf of me. Who cares if I'm serving and you're a guest? Don't let her rattle you. The truth is, I don't mind helping at all. It gives me something to do on Valentine's Day," I said, then added, "Plus ... Derek."

Valentine's Day had lost its blush for me after my fiancé had died two years before. I'd left my job at an estate attorney's office and moved back to Gainesville, Pennsylvania to take a job as a historical tour guide at my Aunt Cecelia's bed-and-breakfast. To complicate matters, Cecelia wasn't really my aunt, but rather my grandma's best friend. But I'd grown up calling her that, and now she was the only family I had left in the world.

So Valentine's Day was a lonely day for me, one that I wanted to cram full of things to help me forget. And serving rich folks fancy food seemed like the perfect chore to take my mind off roses, cupids, and happily-ever-afters.

There was silence on the other end. And then a sigh. "Georgie, I feel so stupid. Now it makes sense. It's just going to be weird sitting there having you serve me."

"Which brings us to the *real* news. You're attending?"

She let out a bark of laughter. "Quit sounding so shocked. Yes! I'm actually one of the guests. I guess Mrs. Vanderton found out we were coming, and that was why she was laying into me, since she knew you were volunteering. It must have been a shock to her system when she discovered commoners would be present at the table."

"I want to hear this. How did you get an invite? Isn't it one of the conditions that you'll write five-figured checks."

4

"I know. I know. Joe got the invite from Mr. Miquel himself. He was the contractor on Mr. Miquel's pool-house remodel job last year."

"That's amazing!" I said, sincerely happy for her. "Are you excited? It's going to be a fancy evening."

"I don't know about excited," she said, but I could hear the smile in her voice. "But we have a babysitter, which is like a twice-a-year event around here. So I plan to whoop it up. Waiter! More wine!" She groaned. "Oh, my gosh. I forgot *you're* the waiter."

"Ha! Don't you worry. I'll keep you glass full."

She took a deep breath and exhaled. "I just wish you'd told me so I didn't feel so blindsided."

"You're making a big deal out of nothing. You know how Mrs. Vanderton is. Nothing makes her happy. The entire town knows that about her."

"She's a bitter, bitter old woman who wears misery like it was a cosmetic."

"Exactly," I said. "So you don't want to kill me anymore? You forgive me?"

"Yeah, I forgive you. Just keep my glass full so I forget I'm having dinner with Mrs. Misery."

"I promise," I said, laughing. "Trust me, it'll be a good time."

Little did I know—not only would I break my promise, but it would be a night the entire town would never forget.

CHAPTER 2

Baker Street Bed and Breakfast had just one set of guests that evening, Mr. and Mrs. Johnson, a retired couple from Topeka, Kansas. They were there specifically to attend the charity dinner.

The night of the dinner, Mr. Johnson cornered me with a forty-minute sit-down on the B&B's couch where he made me scroll through hundreds of pictures of his war memorabilia, pausing at each one to explain the history. His enthusiasm made me smile. To say he was excited to see the sword being displayed at the dinner was an understatement.

Fortunately, his wife—after gently hinting for about ten minutes—flat-out demanded that he get ready for the dinner. He harrumphed, saying it only took him fifteen minutes to dress, while it took her two hours, but he lurched off the couch and went with her.

Cecelia was also volunteering at the charity dinner and had already left for the Miquel manor. Earlier that morning, she'd confided in me that Adele, the caterer in charge of the event, had called in a panic. Apparently, Mrs. Vanderton had gotten wind of the menu and had come unglued on poor Adele over the food choices. Adele was just starting out in the catering business, and being thirty years Mrs. Vanderton's junior, was easily intimidated.

Adele had called Cecelia crying, saying it was much too late to change the menu. Now, Cecelia was softhearted, but she had an iron core. No one was going to get into Cecelia's business and tell her what to do, and she bolstered Adele with that same attitude.

Cecelia had given Adele the same kind of pep talk that I remembered from when I was a kid. When Cecelia had finished talking with me, I'd felt like I could climb Mt. Everest, and the young caterer had felt the same. The menu was six courses, with the main dish being Beef Wellington. For all her hard work, Adele deserved for the dinner to go well.

Mr. and Mrs. Johnson, came down the stairs of the B&B at about half past five, and I admired her red dress and fur stole.

"This was my grandmother's," she said, stroking the fur as Mr. Johnson adjusted his bow tie and slipped into his overcoat.

"You both look lovely!" I said. Then, glancing at the clock on the wall, I realized I was a few minutes late. "I've got to run. I'll see you there!"

Dinner wasn't until eight, but there was wine tasting and a historical presentation at the manor beforehand, where the sword that had been given to John Paulding would be taken from the vault and displayed.

I climbed into my work van, a retired catering vehicle that I fondly called Old Bella. I'll admit, that fondness quickly evaporated on mornings I couldn't get her to start. She was getting a bit more finicky as of late, and I dreaded the moment I had to take her to the garage to get work done. Money had been tight through the Christmas holidays since the B&B's business slowed, but spring was around the corner, and it should pick up soon.

She started right up this time. Just as I was about to shift into gear, my phone rang.

Trying not panic about being late, I dug through my purse for the phone. It was Cecelia.

"Hello?" I said.

"GiGi? Have you left yet?" Her voice sounded anxious as she used my nickname.

"Nope. Still in the driveway."

"Oh good! Can you go grab the pan on the stove for me? I forgot to bring it."

"Absolutely! I'll see you soon." I couldn't help my smile as I undid the seatbelt and scooted out. For once, being a little bit late turned out to save the day.

I jogged up to the front steps and let myself in, sliding to a halt in front of the hall mirror. I'd put my short, dirty-blonde hair in a ponytail while my hair was still damp from the shower, and it now had a ridge sticking up right down the center of my scalp. I took out the rubber band and tried to smooth the ridge down, but it was no use. Sighing, I scooped it back up again and twisted the band in it as I made my way to the kitchen.

The pan was on the stove already covered in foil. I lifted the corner and peeked inside. I had no idea what it was, but a warm vanilla scent rose up, and I breathed in deeply.

Sadly, I tucked the foil down again. None for me. I carried the tray to the van and set it on the floor. After wedging an umbrella against it to keep it from moving, I climbed back into the driver's seat, adjusted the mirror, and stepped on the gas. Old Bella lurched forward with a belch of black smoke.

It was a fifteen minute drive, and by the time I arrived, the manor's driveway was filled with cars. Out at the end, a man dressed as an American Revolutionist waved at me to stop.

I rolled down the window as he came around. "If you could just pull in under the portico, someone there will greet you and park your car."

"Thanks," I said to him, while immediately adding under my breath, "Lovely." Some poor sap was going to have to drive this relic. The van shuddered to the front of the manor and arrived with a backfire. Several valets jumped at the sound, and then laughed, while one looked disgusted.

"At least I know how to make an entrance," I murmured. I opened the door, and a valet handed me a number. His nose wrinkled at the sight of the interior.

"What's your name?" I asked.

He looked at me with surprise. "Robert."

"Robert," I said, straight-faced. "You be careful with my baby. I just had her detailed. Not a scratch."

He stared at me, disbelieving, while I retrieved my tray and a pair of black shoes. Then I followed the walkway around to the back of the manor to the kitchen door.

The inside of the kitchen was bustling when I arrived. Adele was shouting commands while still somehow sounding sweet.

11

Cecelia had her apron on and was buttering rolls to brown in the oven.

I walked over to her with the pan. "How's it going?" I asked, setting it next to her.

"Oh, thank you for grabbing that, GiGi. Well, the guests have been in the drawing room for some time hearing a lecture. Soon, the butler will call them to dinner, so we're just waiting for word that they're seated."

She gestured to a wall where several garment bags hung from a coat rack. "Go get dressed. The restroom is over there."

I hurried to the garments. After searching inside the bags, I finally located a medium and rushed to the bathroom. Quickly, I changed into the plain black dress and white apron. There was a cap, presumably to mimic a 1780s dress code. I undid my ponytail and tied the hat to my head. Then, after slipping on my shoes, I washed my hands and headed out.

"Go refresh the glasses in the drawing room," Adele said when she spotted me. She pressed a bottle of wine in my hand. "It's down the hall to the right. You can't miss it."

I took the bottle, wrapped in a white cloth, and headed out to the drawing room. The manor was huge, feeling even more so with ceilings that stretched two stories above me. The heels of my black loafers clicked against the marble floor that sparkled from overhead chandeliers.

All the doors I passed were closed, but I knew which one was the drawing room. Violin music floated down the hall. I finally came to the heavy oak doors that opened to a luxurious room.

Larger than my whole apartment, the pretentiously cozy room was furnished with red velvet chairs that I assumed were brought in for the event. The presentation was over and the guests were mingling. I recognized our state senator, the meteorologist from our local news station, and the Gainesville mayor.

Pretending I was invisible, I slipped in and went from guest to guest, gesturing to a person's empty glass with my eyes, before tipping in a couple inches of wine and then going to the next.

The French doors were open in the back, allowing entrance to a smaller room filled with several couches. It had a roaring fire going in a natural stone fireplace, and was much cozier, in my opinion, than the other was.

It was there that I found the widow Veronica Vanderton arguing with Gayle Marshall, the wife of the man who owned and rented several buildings to Gainesville's businesses. Gayle and her husband also owned one of the town's antique shops, set apart at the edge of town.

I was about to approach the women when Mrs. Vanderton saw me and waved me off. As I was leaving, I heard Gayle Marshall say, "If you're going to be eavesdropping, don't complain if you don't like what you hear."

"Of course I don't like it. It's unfair and untrue." Mrs. Vanderton snapped back. "I could sue you for libel. You're stressing me out so much, I need my asthma inhaler. What are you trying to do, kill me?"

Back in the main room, I spied Kari and her husband, Joe. They were laughing with the mayor, and it reminded me that despite Joe's good luck in scoring the tickets, Kari really was considered the upper crust in Gainesville society. Her parent's had once owned the manor two doors down, before they sold it to buy a place in Florida and their yacht.

Kari broke away from the men when she saw me. I have to admit, she looked sophisticated in her blue gown.

"Hi!" she said, squeezing my arm. I figured by her smile she'd already had a few glasses of wine.

"More?" I asked, holding up the bottle.

"Oh, no. I really shouldn't. Okay, maybe a little." She giggled, holding out her glass.

I was glad to see her having a good time.

"Hey, you want to go play peacemaker? There's a battle

brewing in the other room." I poured her an extra measure of liquid courage.

"Peacemaker? I'm on it!" She waggled her fingers at Joe and elegantly walked into the other room.

I continued through the party until the bottle was empty. As I headed back down the hallway to the kitchen, I heard footsteps pacing near the foyer. A voice rose in a seething growl. Curiosity got the best of me, so I took a peek.

It was Mr. Miquel, the owner of the manor. I saw his profile before he turned to pace in the other direction. His tanned face looked frustrated, and he had the phone to his ear. Obviously a private phone call.

I backed away, but not before I heard him ask in a voice deep with accusation. "Why didn't you tell me you weren't going to be here? And what do you mean the car broke down? You have a rental?"

Odd. I wonder who was missing, so I hurried to the kitchen where I found Adele looking frazzled. I hated to bug her, but wanted to see if she knew, if for no other reason than Mr. Miquel had been so irritated. "Are all the guests accounted for?," I asked. "Do you have enough meals?"

She nodded. "All the guests are here."

That was puzzling, but then I was caught up in the serving rush.

The next few minutes flew by as Adele inspected the plates as the servers placed on silver trays. The butler came in to inform us that the guests were seated.

"Okay! It's time! Line up, ladies," Adele directed with a clap of her hands.

There were four of us, and we worked in teams—one of us carried the tray on which sat several plated bowls of soup, while the other acted as the server. Penny, a gal I'd recently met at the art studio where I took classes, was working with me.

Adele watched through a crack in the door, while we tried to be as silent as possible. Finally, she nodded and opened the door wide.

We proceeded through like the soup parade. Two extraordinary crystal chandeliers lit the room and in one corner, a stringed quartet softly played. Guests sat, quietly chatting, down both sides of the lavish dining table, and several seemed glad to see us, obviously hungry. Kari gave me a drunken smile and a thumbs up.

As we were walking in, Mr, Miquel clanked on his wine glass to get everyone's attention.

"Thank you, everyone, for joining me tonight. As you can see, my wife is not here." He pointed to an empty place setting next to him. "She had an emergency to attend with her mother. Poor woman had a four-hour drive. She wants you all to know she sends her regrets."

The guests all murmured their condolences.

The line of us servers split, with each pair going down one side of the table. Penny followed me. Carefully, I placed the soup before each guest, trying to hide the sigh of relief at each successful deposit. I was about halfway down when I spotted Mrs. Vanderton. It was hard to miss her. The woman was shaking her head in disapproval as we approached. The jeweled peacock pin she wore in her hair sparkled in the light.

"That woman has on pink nail polish," she hissed loudly to the man seated next to her. "Pink! Can you believe it?"

The man raised his eyebrows.

"You put on an authentic party, you should at least try to dress the part. You should be ashamed." She shook her finger at us.

I didn't know what she was talking about until I saw Penny flush. Her fingers curled under the silver tray as she tried to hide them.

"What's the matter?" A woman across the table asked. I

recognized her as Mrs. Sutter, the mayor's wife and someone who occasionally ran Bingo night down at the Episcopal church.

"I'm just appalled that they forgot to remove their nail polish." Mrs. Vanderton said loudly. "And this woman over there is serving from the left and not the right." She took a sip from her wine glass.

Mrs. Sutter stared at her with pursed lips, clearly not happy with the complaining woman. Their discussion caught the attention of the two people to Mrs. Sutter's right, who were now laughing.

"Is something funny?" Mrs. Vanderton asked loudly. She threw her napkin down on the table.

I swallowed and tried to distract her. "Soup?" I asked.

She stared at the soup with as her forehead wrinkled in suspicion. "What kind is it?"

"Leek with potato," I said.

"And the broth? What is it?"

"Err," I caught the gaze Penny, needing help.

"Chicken broth, ma'am," she answered, her nails still hidden under the tray.

"No seafood, is it? Because I'm allergic to shellfish. Don't make me get my EpiPen. It's in my purse, you know."

"Absolutely not, ma'am," Penny assured her.

Mrs. Vanderton's nose wrinkled as she accepted the bowl. "I don't know about that Adele lady. I tried to tell her, you don't serve potato soup on a night like this. Besides, we've been waiting forever. It's probably cold."

I was very happy to place it in front of her and move on.

In a few minutes, we had everyone served and were sidling back to the kitchen. Soft chatter had resumed around the table. I couldn't help a quick glance back at Mrs. Vanderton. She was pushing items around in her bowl, with deep frown lines around her mouth as if she were stirring dirty laundry rather than soup.

Well, whatever. Having sampled, Adele's cooking at other gatherings, I knew it was first rate.

Back in the kitchen, the chef assistants were arranging trays of bread and plates of salad in preparation for the next course.

"There's no seafood in the soup, is there?" I asked Adele, just to be certain.

She shook her head. "I do have a parchment-wrapped sole as a dinner option for those who don't like Beef Wellington," she said. She puffed her cheeks and blew at a wisp of hair hanging before her eyes.

"Okay, just checking. Someone said they were allergic. We don't want any reactions."

"We absolutely do not," she agreed.

About ten minutes later, Adele assembled us again and sent us back to the dining hall. When I entered this time, Mrs. Vanderton's seat was vacant.

CHAPTER 3

The low hum of several conversations and an occasional subdued laugh filled the dining room and soft violin notes floated through the air. No one seemed to notice Mrs. Vanderton was missing.

Or maybe they just didn't care.

I walked along the table, Penny following me with the silver tray. Carefully, I cleared the plates and stacked them on the tray. At Mrs. Vanderton's, I hesitated, not sure what the protocol was regarding removing a plate from someone who wasn't there.

"Just take it," Penny hissed.

I grabbed it and then continued to clear the table. After a

quick trip into the kitchen to deposit the dishes, we were back out with the second course.

"Wasn't it amazing to see the saber?" Gayle Marshal asked. "All the way from 1782!"

"I'd like to have a second look at it myself," the mayor said. He was a large man, with cheeks like two ham slices. He turned to Mr. Miquel. "Tell the truth. You take it out of the vault and flay it around from time to time."

"You've caught me; It's how I slice my cantaloupes!" Mr. Miquel laughed.

"Don't be greedy, then. Let us play with it," the mayor ribbed him.

"Salad?" I asked, holding out the ice-cold dish.

He nodded with a smile and pushed his cloth napkin away to make a space.

At Mrs. Vanderton's place, I hesitated again. She still was not back. I set the plate down and continued to the next guest.

But when it came time to clear the salad course and Mrs. Vanderton still wasn't back, I felt the first prickle of alarm. Where was she? Had she been so offended by the earlier conversation that she'd left? It was hard for me to imagine. She was such an outspoken woman, it seemed odd she would have gone home without making a scene. Should I try to track the woman down?

Adele eyed the salad when I brought it back. "Someone doesn't like the food? Who's not eating?"

"Mrs. Vanderton," I replied, frowning. "But it's not that she doesn't like it. She's gone."

Adele pressed her lips together. "The woman loves to be the center of attention, so that's surprising. And I'll hold my tongue and not add good riddance."

When it was time to serve the Beef Wellington, I once again had to set the entrée down before an empty chair.

"Do you know where she's at?" I broke protocol and asked the woman who had been sitting on Mrs. Vanderton's right.

The woman glanced at the chair and gave me an empty look. "She just got up and left without a word."

Great. I passed out the main course and then hurried back into the kitchen.

I let Adele know I was going to try to track down Mrs. Vanderton.

Adele asked me, "She's not back?"

I shook my head.

"I don't have time for this." Adele pulled out a tray filled with ramekins. Eyebrows knotted with concentration, she gently set them on the stove so the tops wouldn't crack. Next to her was a butane torch and sugar topping.

My mouth watered at the sight. Creamy, with just a hint of golden brown. I needed to learn how to make them.

Maybe learn how to master cherry pie first, my pessimist side schooled me. I rolled my eyes. I knew how to make cherry pie. I'd just forgotten the sugar that one time.

I walked over to Cecelia. "Did you hear Mrs. Vanderton's missing?"

Cecelia shook her head. Her cheeks were pink from the heat of the kitchen. She was clipping the mint leaves for the crème brûlée. "That woman will do anything for attention."

"Where's the other restroom?" I figured that would be the first place I should look.

"About eight doors down on the left. Be careful not to go in the wrong room. There's an office down that way too."

Great. Watch me break into the private office.

I walked down the long hallway, studying the doors that I passed, searching for the least officey-looking one. Each one was an elegant six-panel of beautiful wood. I gave up and tried number eight, which opened to reveal a velvet lounging

CRÈME BRÛLÉE TO SLAY

couch at the entrance. A true powder room. Around the corner were the sink and toilet.

But the room was empty.

So I guess she did go home. I left the bathroom and walked down to the main entrance. The doorman nodded at me and opened the door.

I stepped outside where I caught Robert, the valet, slumped against the pillar talking into his phone. His face was red with anger. "Don't forget. Ten o'clock tonight."

I cleared my throat to catch his attention. He jumped to his feet and snapped off his phone, only to relax when he saw me in my uniform.

"Robert, did you recently retrieve the car for Mrs. Vanderton?"

He looked at me, his face slack and void of emotion, like he didn't understand what I was saying.

"Mrs. Vanderton? An older lady with curly black hair."

"Oh. Her." His eyebrows flickered. "No, not since she handed me a wet wipe for my hands before I was allowed to park her car."

"Did another valet come get her car?"

"Nah. They're all on break. It's just me out here for the next hour."

I really wanted to press him if he was sure. He must have seen it in my eyes because he jogged over to a board and jingled a key chain at me. "See? Her keys are right here."

I nodded and went back inside. She was still in the manor. Why did that thought freak me out?

I headed for the dining room, holding onto a tiny hope that maybe Mrs. Vanderton was back in her seat. When I saw her seat was still empty, my stomach sunk.

Mr. Miquel was laughing with the mayor, seemingly oblivious to the fact that one of his guests was wandering about his manor unescorted. I hesitated, wondering if I should alert him. Maybe I could find the butler and have him let the owner know discretely.

As I was about to sneak back out, I overheard one of the guests exclaim, "That Vanderton woman is unbelievably rude. I do believe she's left us for good."

"I don't know what she's so high and mighty about. Especially being in such a precarious situation. People in glass houses shouldn't throw stones." Gayle Marshall sniffed.

"Oh, this sounds juicy. Dish it!" said one of the women who'd laughed earlier.

I slowed my retreat and wandered over to the sideboard. There, I folded the wine towel and did a general tidying up, trying to stay inconspicuous.

Gayle Marshall laughed, sounding mean. "I'm just saying, she's not nearly as high and mighty as she pretends. You know she's spent her husband's inheritance, and I've heard"—her voice lowered to a whisper and I strained to listen—"she's going to lose their house."

"No!" One lady gasped.

I glanced up the table at the other guests, wondering what Mr. and Mrs. Johnson thought of all of this. Mr. Johnson was deep in a conversation with the mayor, but Mrs. Johnson seemed to be interested in the gossip. Kari, too, was paying attention.

Gayle Marshall nodded before taking a sip of her wine. She wiped her lips on the linen napkin. "It's true. Veronica is in default."

After a few shocked sighs, another woman added, "That's not all ladies. They say she has a married boyfriend and—"

"All right, let's not get too crazy here." Gayle's voice was crisp as she fluttered her hand and cut the woman off. "I highly doubt that woman could get a man."

There were a few laughs, and then the conversation veered

into a past golf tournament. I refolded the towel and hurried back into the kitchen.

Adele was arranging her crème brûlée on trays. She wiped a pan and tweaked a mint leaf, then turned to stare at us.

"Everyone line up! This is the grand finale," she shouted. Penny picked up the tray and followed me as we left to pass out desserts. Behind us was the sommelier who would bring around a light moscato to pair with the dessert.

The gossip seemed to have died down around the table. Good-natured teasing came from several of the men as they tried to convince Mr. Miquel to let them play with the sword. By the time I'd made it around the table, it appeared they were wearing him down.

Fifteen minutes later, the guests were finished and pushing back from the table. Complaining good-naturedly about full bellies, the men followed Mr. Miquel, presumably back to the drawing room.

The women collected by the door, and I wondered if they would continue the old-fashioned tradition of men and women separating. Slowly, the women trickled from the dining room as well.

When everyone had left, I began to stack the dessert dishes while someone else collected the wine glasses. Penny and I smiled at each other, relieved to have pulled off the huge dinner without a major incident. I rolled my neck to release tension.

"That was quite an experience," Penny said. She glanced at her fingernails, probably still stunned at the problems the manicure had given her earlier.

"You ready to do it again?" I asked, teasing.

"Wow, you're so not full of good ideas," she answered. "I'm pretty sure I'm swearing off this catering business."

As I hefted the tray to carry it back to the kitchen, a woman's scream ripped through the house.

I dropped the tray on the table and ran from the room to see what was happening.

"The police! Call the police!" A woman reeled down the hallway, screaming. She caught my arm as I tried to pass. "Get help!" she yelled, her fingernails digging in to my flesh.

I shook her off and ran down the hall. My lungs were tight and my heart pounding as I took the left and dashed up the hallway. Two doors down from the drawing room, a crowd of people stood outside the doorway.

They each had different degrees of horror on their face. Kari had hers buried into her husband's shoulder. Gayle Marshall held her hand over her mouth. The mayor stood in the corner as if trying to disassociate himself.

I slowed my steps, not sure I wanted to see what they were staring at.

Because I knew.

Of course I knew. There could only be one thing that would cause such a reaction.

Mr. Miquel rushed into the room from behind me, knocking shoulders with me as he passed. I followed after him as if an invisible wake were pulling me along.

Slowly, I looked around the corner and inside.

The room appeared to be a large study. Mrs. Vanderton was lying on her stomach inside the entrance, arms and legs sprawled out across the floor. Mr. Miquel rolled her over, against the pleas and shrieks from a few of the women begging him to not move her. But after Mrs. Vanderton turned face up, we all saw that no amount of rolling would hurt her condition. Blue lips and a swollen face. I closed my eyes at the sight, horrified.

The guests backed away from the door, leaving just Mr. Miquel kneeling by her side. He stroked her cheek and then covered his eyes. I watched him take several deep breaths. Wearily, he stood up.

Someone must have called the police. Time seemed to be standing still, but all of a sudden, officers were there. They shuffled us to the end of the hall, and I was surprised to see Gayle Marshall still crying. It seemed an odd reaction after their recent fight.

The paramedics almost strolled through, not with a sense of urgency like they normally do. Mics squawked and codes were called in, all at a leisurely pace.

I wanted to know what happened. Had she choked? Why come all the way down the hall to this room if she'd been choking? During my first aid class, somebody had mentioned that choking people sometimes went to the bathroom to hide because of shame, so it wasn't out of the question.

But was Veronica Vanderton really someone like that? Someone who'd rather hide than get help in the face of unflattering body movements?

I thought about the gossip that had salaciously come out over the dinner table—the fact that her house was about to be foreclosed on, and her inheritance was gone. And I remembered that brightly colored jeweled peacock she'd had pinned in her hair. She definitely fit the bill of someone who cared about what people thought of her, right down to the flash of jewelry in the face of rumored bankruptcy.

"If I could have you all move into there," one of the officers said. He guided all of us to the next room, which turned out to be the library.

The room was loaded from floor to ceiling with books. Normally the sight would have caused butterflies in my stomach and frozen my steps as I tried to take in all the beautiful treasures. But now, I didn't spare the books a second glance. Instead, I studied all the guests for their reactions.

Several table lamps shone warm light throughout the room, the light reflecting off the polished wood wainscoting. From the base of the trim board to the ceiling were bookshelves, each filled to capacity. The oak floors were covered with thick wool rugs, and several of the guests settled down onto the few scattered couches. One of the women held a throw pillow as if unsure of where to set it. Kari stood in the corner with Joe, fiercely whispering into her phone. I just caught one of the words, "babysitter."

The local meteorologist leaned against the doorframe. Like so many others, he had his phone out, his thumbs flying across the screen.

There was a long table against one of the walls holding a tray with a decanter of some dark liquid and a plate of cookies. One of the women who'd laughed at Mrs. Vanderton earlier headed toward them. She scooped up a cookie and shoved it into her mouth, her eyes furtively looking around.

"What?" she asked around the cookie when she caught Joe watching.

"Nothing." He shrugged.

"I'm stress eating. Just leave me alone." She grabbed another cookie and walked to the other side of the room.

I understood stress eating, but not when there was a dead body in the other room. My stomach roiled at the thought and I had to turn away.

Two officers wandered in our group, asking basic questions like, "What happened?" and "when did she leave the table?"

I heard a squeak and knew it was the gurney. The paramedics passed by the open doorway on their way to the front door. A blanket covered Veronica's face. My stomach went from roiling to flat-out rebellion. I held my hand over my mouth looking for a distraction, anything. Spotting a painting, I wandered over to it.

The painting was abstract, with a lot of green and blue splotches, but it reminded me of the water under a bridge where I liked to play as a girl. I'd dangle my legs over the edge and look for minnows. Breathing deeply, I tried to imagine that place.

Finally, my heart stopped pounding, and the nausea eased. Kari came over and gave me a hug. The police seemed to be finishing up, and after a few more questions, they said we were free to leave.

Several sighs of relief hissed through the air at the news and the crowd filtered out, the mayor leading the way.

I was not so free because I still had to finish cleaning the kitchen. There was a note on the counter from Adele thanking us for our help. Both she and Cecelia had already left by the time Penny and I made it back there. Everything they'd brought to cater was gone, but the items belonging to the house were still there.

I filled a plastic tub with soapy water and began to wash wine glasses. Penny joined me with a towel. I handed her a glass, and she started wiping.

"Can you believe she's gone?" I asked.

"It's surreal. She was like the embodiment of bitterness one minute and dead the next." She shook her head.

"It's sad. I bet she had a calendar filled with appointments. She had plans and goals." I rinsed another glass and handed it to her.

"Why is that sad?"

I shrugged. "I don't know. Just that it was so unexpected. Makes me feel bad."

"What do you think happened to her?" Penny asked.

I bit my lip, remembering that face. "I guess she must have choked."

"Choked on what? The soup?" Her voice sounded incredulous.

That was true. It did sound weird when I thought about it that way. "Maybe on a bit of potato?" I suggested.

"Maybe," Penny agreed with a shrug of her shoulders.

I continued to wash and pass them to her to dry. Then, together we polished and packed the glasses. Meanwhile, my thoughts were running on overtime. How could you choke on a bit of potato? Wouldn't you cough first? But no one had noticed if she had a problem when she left the table.

My thoughts were running deep, and I was just about to reach a conclusion when another yell broke the relative quietness of the house, this time from a man. Startled, I jumped and screamed myself.

"Call the police!" the man yelled. "I've been robbed!"

CHAPTER 4

I ran, with Penny at my heels, in the direction of the man's hysterical shrieks. My heart pounded as the sound led us in the same direction where we'd just found Mrs. Vanderton not an hour before. But instead of coming from the study at the end of the hall, the bellowing led us to the drawing room.

I walked in slowly, my hand trailing on the backs of the velvet chairs that had been set up for the presentation. Up front was the same cloth-draped table. But the sword that had been displayed there like the crown jewel was missing. Mr. Miquel stared down at the table with his mouth open and his eyes wild. His hands hung limp and powerless at his sides.

"Mr. Miquel?" I called, concerned.

He turned stiffly, as though he were a wind-up toy on its last few winds. His eyes were red rimmed and his hand reached to clench his chest. He staggered back against the table.

"Mr. Miquel!" I said, more urgently. Was he having a heart attack? "Are you okay?"

I hadn't heard her come in, but Gayle zipped past me. She must have thought the same thing. "Steve! Are you okay? What's wrong? Steve? Answer me!"

He reeled on his feet, the table failing to help him keep balance. I ran over and grabbed his arm to steady him. Together, Gayle and I helped him across the room and into one of the chairs.

I scrambled for my phone from my apron pocket and dialed Frank. He was Cecelia's grandson, and my old childhood friend. He came back to Gainesville after retiring from the Army about six months before I returned. We reconnected as two adults both trying to survive some past trauma. And now, our friendship was better than it had ever been.

"You okay?" he asked, forgoing the hello.

"Frank, It's been a crazy night, We—"

"Yea, I know. I've been following on the scanner."

"Well, we need the police again. I think Mr. Miquel needs an ambulance. He—" I glanced down at him. His coloring wasn't too good, the shade of gray that made me want to tell Frank to hurry. I turned away from Mr. Miquel and said in a low voice, "He may be having a heart attack. He's just found out he's been robbed. Someone took his antique sword—the one the whole dinner was about. It's missing."

"You're kidding me!" Frank whistled through his teeth. "Anyone else call this in?"

I turned around and found Penny, who had her phone to her ear. "Maybe? I really don't know."

"Okay, I'll get on the horn and be right down."

I hung up, feeling a rush of reassurance just from knowing he was on his way. I'd really missed him when he hadn't come with the first wave of police.

"I'm fine, love." Mr. Miquel waved off Gayle, who was offering him a glass of water. "I just can't believe it. Why is this happening?" He stared again at the table as if expecting to find out it was some cruel trick and the sword would reappear.

"Do you have any security cameras set up?" I asked.

He shook his head. "Not in this room. Only in the study, where I keep it locked in its case. Of course, we have cameras at the entrance and all the other exits."

"Okay, good. Don't worry. The police will be able to track the thief down through them. It will be okay, I promise," I said, trying to sound more sure than I felt.

He looked at me like he was a drowning man, just hoping for a lifeline. "I can't believe this has happened. I'm not going to recover."

"The police will find it. I'm sure it'll be just a matter of looking at the video."

He groaned and his head dropped. "What a night. What I held dear, gone."

I backed away, not wanting to intrude on his pain any longer, and walked over to Penny. She'd never gone past the doorway, and was leaning against the frame, watching from a distance.

"Girl," she whispered as I approached.

"I know. I can't even believe it, either," I whispered back. "You didn't happen to see anything weird lately, did you?"

She stared at me like I was crazy. "Weirder than the body of one of the guests that I'd just served dinner to?"

I grimaced and rubbed my forehead. "Yeah. Besides that."

She shook her head. "No. Did you?"

I shook my head. By now the butler had arrived and stood next to us. His gaze swept across the empty table to his boss sitting in the front row with his head in his hands. The butler's nostrils flared as he sighed.

"Have the police been called, ma'am?" he asked me.

"Yes," I said. "They're on their way. Along with an ambulance, I think. Mr. Miquel was not doing too well a minute ago."

He nodded and briskly walked up to him. From inside his jacket, he pulled out a silver vial, which he handed to Mr. Miquel.

Mr. Miquel slowly lifted his head and then accepted the vial. He unscrewed the top and slipped something from inside into his mouth, and then nodded grimly in thanks.

The police arrived and quickly demarked the crime scene with yellow tape and the entrance to the room was cordoned off. It was surreal when they pulled Penny and me aside and questioned us again, this time more thoroughly. Detective Kirby, a police officer who'd been on the first scene, asked me what I'd been doing since they'd left earlier, and I explained that I'd been washing dishes. Obviously, Penny collaborated.

I was so happy to see Frank, although he stayed on the outskirts. Since he wasn't dressed in uniform, I assumed he wasn't on duty. As soon as Detective Kirby finished questioning me, I headed over to him.

"I guess I need to keep a closer eye on you," Frank said with one eyebrow raised. "Apparently, you're a trouble magnet."

I made a face at him, a little perturbed that it sounded like he was only half-joking.

The forensic team brushed passed the two of us and began setting up their equipment while a paramedic checked Mr. Miquel out.

Frank glanced toward the distressed man. "I'll be right back," he told me.

"Okay," I said, trudging toward the front door. "I'm going to have my van brought up front." I turned wearily for the front door.

The doorman was there, looking as polite as ever as he opened the door for me. Outside, I found Penny standing and shivering, while she waited for them to bring her car around.

"Crazy night," she chattered while hugging herself. A blue car came down the driveway, and Robert got out.

"I'll see you later," she said as she hurried down the stairs to her vehicle.

Robert jogged up the stairs to get my number. He gave me a wink, but a clearing of a throat stopped the valet cold. Unbeknownst to me, Frank had followed after me and now stared down at him. Robert ducked his head and hurried to his booth.

I was tired and leaned against Frank's shoulder when his arm snaked around me and pulled me close. He smelled like clean soap.

So far, we hadn't defined what we were doing together. All I knew was that it felt good.

It was nice to have someone who was trustworthy and stable in my life.

"So, how are you doing, Short Stuff?" he said roughly into my hair.

I chuckled softly at the old nickname he'd called me as a kid. Stable was definitely the word for him. Some things never changed.

"I'm tired. Honestly, all I can think about is that poor woman. The fact that there's been a sword stolen hasn't even sunk in yet."

"Poor woman. Hmm. That might be the first time those two words were ever used to refer to her," he said dryly.

"Frank! That's so mean. What an awful way to go." I shivered and rubbed my arms. I was still in my server's uniform, and the cold air ripped through the thin fabric.

"I hear you. But, she was just so nasty. I'll never forget how she treated my grandma."

I nodded. When Cecelia had purchased the Baker Street Bed and Breakfast, Mrs. Vanderton had made it her goal to try to get the city to deny Cecelia's business permit on the grounds that the house was unsafe. While Cecelia was a family friend and not blood, I felt as protective of her as Frank did about anyone messing with her.

Then it came to light that Mrs. Vanderton had originally tried to buy it, herself. But the owners had chosen to sell it to Cecelia instead. I'm sure it stung Mrs. Vanderton, especially since Cecelia's offer was several thousand less than her own.

It seemed to prove that money didn't always make up for bad behavior.

I could hear my van's coughing approach before I saw the vehicle.

"You might need to get that to the garage," Frank said, lifting his eyebrows as the van backfired.

I nodded and sighed. One more thing on my plate, and my bills were mounting up. I'd just barely managed to scrape up rent for the month.

Frank must have noticed my stress. "It'll be okay," he said, giving me another squeeze as the valet pulled the van up to the steps.

"Call me if you hear anything," I said, and then walked down to the van and climbed in.

Honestly, the smell of barbecue saturated into the fibers of the old catering vehicle felt welcoming and homey as I climbed in.

I was so ready to be done with the day, and hoped it was done with me, too.

CHAPTER 5

The next morning, I shot out of bed when the alarm went off. I'd been dreaming that I was serving dinner at a never-ending table of zombies.

I clutched the side of the table as my heart pounded in my chest. *Where am I? It's okay. No dead bodies.* Quickly, I fumbled with the button to shut off the alarm. My head was still foggy as I headed to the bathroom.

Like a punch, I remembered Mrs. Vanderton.

And the sword.

Ay yi yi. You just couldn't make that stuff up. I took a quick shower, and then got ready to leave for the B&B.

Outside was bathed in a cool, gray light from the overcast sky.

Snow had fallen during the night, leaving everything white and fresh that February morning. Old Bella hummed along, while I held a hand over the heater vent. She might have her quirks, but she could blast out heat better than any car I'd ever driven before, and I happily soaked it in.

I walked into the B&B just in time to see Cecelia taking down the hanging heart garland.

"Good riddance," I muttered under my breath. The only benefit I could see about Valentine's Day was all the candy that went on clearance the day after. And then a little louder, I added, "Good morning!"

"Hello!" she chimed back in that happy voice of hers. "Can you believe the snow?"

"Well, I for one, am glad we're heading back to eighty-degree weather tomorrow," Mr. Johnson said as the married couple came down the stairs.

"Good morning!" Cecelia told them. "We're having French toast with homemade applesauce. Is there anything else I can make you for breakfast?"

"No," Mrs. Johnson said, shaking her head. "French toast will be lovely."

"Okay, then," Cecelia said, motioning toward the dining room. "Go have a seat and I'll bring your coffee right out."

I followed her into the kitchen and grabbed the carafe and tray of cream. Back in the dining room, I saw that Cecelia had already set the table with flowers, syrup, jam, and a newspaper. It all looked cozy in the early morning light.

"Good morning," I said, filling their mugs. "How'd you sleep after last night?"

Mrs. Johnson shook her head and blew on her coffee. "That poor, poor woman."

I realized then that they didn't know about the sword being stolen, since they'd left right before it was discovered missing. I decided not to mention it.

"Did you know her?" Mrs. Johnson asked.

"No, actually I didn't. I've only been back in town for a little over a year. But she was pretty well known, from what I've heard."

"She seemed to have quite a reputation," Mrs. Johnson said.

Her husband jumped in to agree. "I'd say so. Did you see how they went after her at dinner?"

"They did?" I asked.

"Yeah, just before she left the table. That Gayle lady kept poking her with rude comments. I honestly thought she was leaving because she was offended, not that she was choking."

"Mark!" Mrs. Johnson looked horrified.

He lifted an eyebrow. "Sorry for being blunt. That's what happened, though."

"It's just terrible she didn't ask for help." Mrs. Johnson shook her head.

"I agree," I said. Stalling for time, I rearranged the breakfast condiments on their tray. "Did you see anything that stood out to you last night? Like, did anyone else leave the dinner?"

"Well, we did see Mr. Miquel leave the presentation."

I was surprised. "You did? About what time?"

"His phone rang as he was walking up to the podium." Mrs. Johnson looked to her husband for confirmation. "Remember, honey? He left just before it was supposed to start. He was back about ten minutes later."

Her husband nodded. "Yes, that's right. He did leave for a few minutes. I didn't think anything about it. I just used it as an excuse to get my wine glass refilled."

Mrs. Johnson smiled. "You were having a good time, that's for sure."

It reminded me of how I'd seen Mr. Miquel talking on his phone later. *Who was he waiting for? Did the phone call have to do with that?*

"Did you get a chance to look at the sword? What'd you think?" I asked, thinking of how Mr. Johnson loved American Revolution relics.

"Yes, and it was beautiful. Good, solid American brass hilt with a lion-head pommel and wooden grips."

I realized I hadn't even gotten a chance to see it. That thought bummed me out.

"I still can't believe that happened to that poor woman," Mrs. Johnson pursed her lips. "You know, it reminds me of something I saw when I was a child. We'd just left church and were at a little diner in our town."

"You saw someone choke?" I asked.

"Yes, I suppose so. At the time, I didn't know she was choking. No one did. We were celebrating my father's birthday. Oh that was years ago. Anyway, a woman who was seated at the table across from us suddenly stood up and hurried to the bathroom. It came out later that she'd been choking and had actually died in there."

"Oh, how awful," I said. "That must have really scarred you as a child."

Her eyebrows pulled together as she seemed to be trying to remember. "I don't recall being traumatized. I was a rather analytical child. Instead, I tried to figure out why she'd left instead of getting help. I simply couldn't understand why someone would rather hide away than to chance making a scene. But then, I suppose I watched it happen again last night."

Something about what she said stuck out to me. It was the same thought I'd had the night before. There *were* people in the world who'd rather die than make a scene. But Mrs. Vanderton was a woman who lived to make a scene.

Cecelia came in bearing two plates full of French toast, as well as a platter of ham, sausage, and bacon.

"All right, my lovelies. I hope you enjoy breakfast," she said as she set them down. After a moment, she turned one plate so that it would look more pleasing, and then smiled at her guests.

I hurried into the kitchen to get the glass pitcher of orange juice. As I pulled it from the refrigerator, my phone rang.

I answered it. "Hello?"

It was Frank. "You have time to talk?"

"Give me a minute. I'll call you back."

I hung up and took the juice out to the dining room and filled the glasses. Mr. and Mrs. Johnson were enjoying the food with eye rolls of delight. I completely understood their reaction. Cecelia was a darn good cook.

Back in the kitchen, I dialed up Frank as I returned the pitcher to the fridge.

"Hi Frank. What's up?" I said when he answered.

He was as blunt as he ever was. "We have the cause of death. Anaphylactic shock."

"Oh my gosh." She hadn't choked. She'd died of an allergic reaction. I rubbed the goosebumps on my arm as I remembered our conversation when I'd brought her the soup.

"Forensics is going to need samples of all the food." He exhaled heavily. "Also, Detective Kirby will want to talk with you since you're the one who served her."

The goosebumps now ran down my spine. "Am I a suspect?" I swallowed, my mouth dry.

He cleared his throat. "I don't think so. At this time, they're running the investigation as if it was an accidental death. So, there are no suspects. But one of the dinner guests gave a statement that Mrs. Vanderton specifically asked you if there was seafood in the food, so you'll probably be questioned about that."

"She did ask. And I went in to the chef to double-check that there was absolutely no seafood in the dish I served her."

"Was that the only allergy she mentioned? Not nuts or anything else?"

"Yes. That was it. She was very adamant, but the only seafood we had on the menu was sole, and that was by special order." I paused for a moment. "Was she on her way to get her EpiPen from her purse? She mentioned she carried one there."

"I'm not sure why she was in the study. Anyway, we notified the next of kin, which turns out to be a sister from Orlando. A Mrs. Amelia Spalding. She's flying up tomorrow morning."

"Oh how sad. Were you the one who had to inform her? Were they close?"

He let out a grunt and I could imagine he was probably rubbing his face the way that he did when he was mentally tired. "Yeah. Just got off the phone with her. Oddly, the sister mentioned she hadn't talked to Mrs. Vanderton in nearly two years."

"Wow." I was surprised, even though maybe I shouldn't have been. Mrs. Vanderton had seemed to repel most of the town's people. I guess I could see how she'd have done the same to her family.

"Do you know if that was all the family she had left?" I asked.

"There's a brother too. Apparently he is out of the country. Mrs. Spalding assured me that she'd find a way to get into contact with him."

"Hmm, definitely not a close family then."

"No, apparently not. So, I have some other not-so-great news. Apparently, Detective Kirby found a can of shrimp meat in the bottom of the kitchen trash."

I gasped. "It must have been from a meal they had earlier. Maybe the trash hadn't been removed for a few days?

"Maybe." He didn't sound convinced.

I thanked him and hung up, sighing. Honestly, I was not looking forward to a third interview with the police in less than twenty-four hours.

CHAPTER 6

The interview took place an hour later and was much easier than I'd expected. Rather than meet again in person, Detective Kirby called me, asking basic questions about exactly what had happened when I served Mrs. Vanderton. Seemingly satisfied, he ended the conversation in less than five minutes.

The Johnsons had plans, today so, with no guests staying for lunch, Cecelia had reluctantly had me go home. There was no use paying me to stay when there was no work.

I called Kari to talk about last night, and she invited me for a short jog around the block. I should have been more suspicious, but I was feeling guilty for my lack of commitment to my resolutions. I'd started the new year with a promise to myself that I'd exercise for at least forty minutes every day.

Well, that had worked for the first three days. But by day four, my muscles were so sore, I had to take a break. Since then, my workouts had been pretty spotty. It really made me rethink why I even bothered to make New Year's resolutions, if I wasn't going to keep them.

Still, I was here now, despite the slush on the ground. As the coldness seeped in through the soles of my sneakers, I was pretty sure I could have worked the snow as an excuse for not going, if I'd really wanted to. The fact that I didn't made me proud of my dedication.

Kari came to the door in her yoga clothes, blonde hair in a high ponytail, looking as chipper as ever.

"Hey, how are you?" I moved back and forth on my feet, trying to warm up. My tennis shoes squelched in the slush.

"I'm good. Tired. Maybe a hint of a headache." With that comment, she just out-dedicated my dedication. "How are *you* doing?" she asked as she shut the front door and locked it.

"Good, tired. Never want to do another catering event again." I thought about it. "Although the person who made it so unpleasant ended up dying so...."

She laughed and rolled her eyes. "So there is that. Ahh, poor Veronica Vanderton. What a legacy she left, huh?"

"It certainly doesn't seem like she's going to be missed much, which is kind of sad."

"That is sad. Besides, no one deserves to go out like that."

"Like what? Choking?" I asked.

"Exactly."

"Well," I hesitated. I knew I shouldn't tell her, but she was my best friend. And Frank hadn't said to keep it a secret. "I've just received some news. She didn't choke."

"What?" Kari's blue eyes rounded. "Are you serious? What happened?"

"She ate something she was allergic to. She died of anaphylactic shock."

"Oh, how horrible." Kari stretched her legs. Her voice was muffled as she bent toward her toes. "I remember her mentioning at dinner how she couldn't eat shellfish. But there wasn't any, was there?"

"No. I even checked with Adele just to be sure."

"Wow. That's weird." She checked her wrist where she wore a step tracker. "Okay, you ready?"

We jogged the first block, with me feeling like a Shetland pony shambling along next to a thoroughbred.

Not everyone is meant to look elegant all the time. I came down hard and nearly twisted my ankle. *And maybe not even some of the time.*

We jogged several more blocks with no end in sight. The slush made soft splats with each step. A familiar pinch started in my side, and I groaned. I'd always been susceptible to those side cramps, even as a kid. As it grew stronger, I remembered why I didn't like to jog.

Painting's exercise, I told myself. *And cooking*—pant, pant—*cooking is exercise too. All that dough rolling. Wrists of steel!*

By the time we arrived at the park, the stitch in my side was unbearable.

"I need ... to ... slow down," I gasped. I eased up until I was taking turtle steps behind her.

"You did good, super good." Ever the cheerleader, Kari tried to rally me. But there was no rallying at that point, and I reeled over to one of the benches to sit. I didn't even care about the puddles on the seat from melting snow.

Kari stood before me and stretched her legs. "That was fun!"

I couldn't help but smile. Even her voice was spirited. "So

about the dinner last night. You didn't see anything weird happen?"

"Nope. Not a thing."

"Because you're not going to believe this, but someone used Vanderton's death as a distraction to swipe the sword."

"What? Are you kidding me?" Her mouth hung open. She retwisted her hair back up into a ponytail. "That thing was a landmark for Gainesville. It's practically our mascot." She thought about it for a second, and then indignantly added, "It *is* our mascot! It's carried by the trooper bear on the high school banner!"

I nodded, remembering. That's right. There was a bear drawing a sword on the red flag.

"Do you have any ideas about who could have stolen it?" I asked. I couldn't see how she would, but it didn't hurt to ask.

"Well, there was that one lady who left during the dinner. It was a few minutes after Mrs. Vanderton disappeared."

My jaw dropped. "You're the first one to mention this. Who was it?"

"She's the gal wearing that a red hat. The one with the big plume."

I blinked, not sure what to think. She'd just described Mrs.

Johnson. "Yeah, I know who she is. She's a guest at the Baker Street Bed and Breakfast. But I don't remember her leaving during the meal."

"It was after you brought the salad. She excused herself for a moment. I didn't think anything of it until you asked just now."

I rubbed my temple. What did this mean? Did Mrs. Johnson see Mrs. Vanderton? But wouldn't she have raised the alarm? "I'll be seeing her later. I guess I need to ask her about it."

"Okay, but keep me in the loop, because I want to know. Don't be holding anything back after I've just given you a good scoop." She eyed me hopefully as I sat there. "You ready to get going?"

"I'm ready to get going, but I'm done running." I laughed. "I really should head back to the bed and breakfast. It's kind of slow lately, but maybe Cecelia will need me to help with dinner."

Kari tightened her shoelaces. "All right. Tomorrow then?"

I stood up and nearly wept at the way my muscles protested. "I don't know about that. We'll see."

Kari smiled. "Drink lots of water. You'll be okay. I'm not giving up on you."

59

As I limped back to Kari's house where I'd left my car, I texted Adele.

—How are you doing?

I had a feeling that by now she'd heard about the allergic reaction. I'm sure the police had already questioned her.

There were bubbles as though she were typing back. And then my phone rang.

It was Adele.

"Hey lady," I answered. "How are you?"

There was a long silence.

"Adele?" I asked.

CHAPTER 7

I drove to Adele's house, my mind spinning. The poor woman had sounded like a wreck on the other end of the phone. I could scarcely understand a word she'd said, it was so broken up with sobs and gulps of air. Finally, I told her to hang in there, and that I was on my way.

The local doughnut shop's sign flashed at me. Fresh doughnuts! I pulled in and ordered several different ones. That way, I could come bearing gifts. And hardly anyone could refuse the gift of a fresh doughnut.

They were warm, and their sweet smell filled the van as I set the box on the passenger seat. Following the map on my phone, I drove the six blocks to her home.

It was a small house, yellow, with white clapboard trim. Carrying the box, I walked to the front door and knocked.

She answered the door in her bathrobe, her hair pulled back into a messy bun. Her eyes were red and puffy.

"Oh, Adele," I said, immediately juggling the box to give her a hug.

"Georgie! This is awful! They found a shrimp can. They're saying it was my fault!" That declaration started her sobbing in full force again.

I released her and scooted her in, then closed the door behind me. "We're going to figure this out. Everyone who worked with you last night knows you didn't have shellfish on the menu."

"It doesn't matter," she wailed. "It's not the police or the investigation I'm worried about. It's my reputation. My business is brand new and already I'm going to be labeled a guest killer!"

"No, no, you aren't," I said, trying to soothe her. But what did I know? Gossip could be like a brutal feral animal tearing into lives. Still, I'd do everything I could to protect her. I led her to her kitchen. The sink and counters were overflowing with dirty dishes. I started searching the cupboards for a coffee mug.

"What are you looking for?" she sniffed.

"I'm going to make you a nice cup of tea to go with these doughnuts. And then we are going to figure this out."

She gave me a few directions, and I soon set a steaming cup of mint tea before her. I really wanted to give her chamomile, since that was especially soothing, but at least mint wasn't caffeinated. I pulled out a chair across from her and opened the box of doughnuts.

"So, what's you pleasure? I grabbed a variety," I said. "Sprinkles? Buttermilk? Or a maple twist?"

She smiled and reached in to break the buttermilk in half. "You didn't have to do this." She sniffed and wiped her nose on her sleeve.

"Pish. It was just as much for me. I earned this. After all, I did go jogging today." I had the other half of the doughnut. Adele grabbed her mug and I waited to ask any questions until she took a sip.

"Okay, so the police contacted you?" I asked.

She nodded, her mouth full of doughnut.

"And what did you tell them?"

She swallowed and then brushed a wisp of hair from her face. "I gave them my menu and the list of all the ingredients I used. I insisted the canned shrimp wasn't mine. They even collected my grocery list for evidence."

"Okay, good. Did you give them the names of everyone who helped you prepare the meal?"

She nodded, cupping her mug like it was a life preserver.

"It simply did not come from you. I know that." I sat back in the chair, thinking. "The canned shrimp had nothing to do with you. It could have even been from the night before. Now, was there any other food that you set out?"

"We had hors d'oeuvres earlier in the evening, before the presentation. Prosciutto-wrapped baby asparagus, phyllo cups with ricotta chèvre and pancetta, and cherry-tomato pepper tartlets."

Some of those names were unfamiliar to me. "None of those include seafood, though, right?"

She shook her head.

Not that it really mattered if they did, because there was too much time between the appetizers and the time of Veronica's death for it to be the dramatic type of anaphylactic shock that she'd suffered.

I thought of something else. "Did you set out any dessert or finger foods for the guests to eat as they mingled?"

She shook her head. "Just the opening wine and hors d'oeuvres. And then we served dinner."

"I see. Well, I remember one of the guests eating a cookie in the library. There was a big plate of them. You're sure that wasn't from you?"

"Definitely not. I didn't bring any cookies. We had the crème brûlée for dessert."

"Yes, I remember." What was I even thinking? Shrimp cookies? I hardly could imagine so. But it *was* odd they were sitting out. Maybe they'd somehow been cross-contaminated. Even poisoned? I needed to get the info to Frank as soon as possible. Hopefully, the cookies were still available for some kind of testing.

Adele seemed curious with my line of questioning. "The fact that you saw cookies proves there was other food available. Food I didn't prepare. Georgie! This could be my saving grace!"

I grabbed my phone, deciding to text Frank the information right away. "I completely agree, and you never know. She may have suffered from a nut allergy as well."

She sat back, looking so much more hopeful. I was, too, even though I had to squelch that tiny inner voice reminding me Mrs. Vanderton wasn't found in the library where the cookies were, but in the study. But perhaps she'd taken her cookie in there to eat.

"Don't you worry," I said. "We're going to get the word out. If I have to print up flyers and plaster them around town announcing how the accident happened, I will. We're not going to let anything happen to your business. We've got your back."

She took another sip of her tea and gave a big sigh. Suddenly interested in the doughnuts again, she grabbed another piece.

As she ate it, she glanced around her kitchen. "Good grief. What a mess."

While I waited for Frank to reply to my text, I thought back to what Kari said about Mrs. Johnson leaving the dinner, and about that shrimp can. Were they both just coincidences?

Exploring the origins of the cookie and whether or not she had a nut allergy seemed like the right way to go. I could explain those other clues away, couldn't I?

CHAPTER 8

rank still hadn't responded to my text by the time I left Adele's. I headed to the B&B, hoping it wasn't too late to test those cookies. I wanted them to be the answer so badly.

The clouds had burned off, and the slush had nearly melted away since this morning, leaving wet mucky puddles that reflected the sunlight in brilliant white laser waves. I fumbled for my sunglasses in the cup holder and slid them on.

Despite the setback of the snowstorm, I was holding out hope for an early spring. It had been a long, gray winter, and my skin felt like it was jumping for joy at the sunshine warming it through the window.

I drove down Baker Street and pulled into the B&B's

driveway. The Johnson's car was there, which was good news for me. Maybe I could get to the bottom of why she'd left during dinner.

I parked the van and climbed out. As I walked down the driveway, a high-pitched barrage of barking arrested me in my tracks.

Peanut.

She streaked out from under the bushes and toward me, her tongue hanging out. Normally, I would have dropped to my knees to welcome her, but my mouth dropped instead. The fawn-colored Pomeranian was black with mud, her fur slicked back like a seal's.

"Oh my—"

Her intense, happy yipping cut me off. I frantically looked around for Oscar O'Neil, her owner and our next door neighbor. She danced at my feet on her back legs as her front paws scrabbled against my pants in a plea to pick her up.

There was no sight of the crotchety old man.

A bad feeling crept over me. "Come on, Peanut."

Oscar was intent on calling the pup Bear, but the dog never answered to it, and I was in no mood to play name games today. Best just to call her Peanut, the name Oscar's late wife had bestowed on the pup.

I walked across the squishy yard and down my neighbor's driveway. He wasn't in sight, which was rare. The dog was never outside without him unless she'd escaped.

I knocked on the door. After several minutes and harder knocks, it became apparent he wasn't coming to the door. That meant he had to be outside, somewhere. I eyed the muddy yard, the conditions of which grew worse around the side to the back. There was nothing for it. Groaning, I picked my way around the worst of the mud puddles to go search for Peanut's owner.

"Mr. O'Neil!" I yelled. "Oscar!"

"What are you caterwauling about? I'm back here," called the grumpy voice that I'd grown to love. He may be a bit prickly, but through the months of walking Peanut, I was getting to know the teddy bear he was on the inside.

His arthritis kept him from walking the dog, but you'd never hear a whisper of that from him. No, in his eyes, he was still the same hardened man that he'd always been. It made me wonder what he'd done for a living before he'd retired. I'd have to ask him, one time.

I came around the corner to see him nearly knee deep in mud. He looked at me with a scowl, but I saw relief on his craggy, old face.

"What are you doing out here, Oscar?" I said, trying to pick my way over to him.

He'd sunk to nearly the top of his rubber boots. Mud was smeared across his arms and legs like he'd fallen at least once, fighting to get out.

"What do you think I'm doing?" he snapped. "Checking my boots for holes?" He struggled forward again, arms waving, but his feet were stuck tight.

"Okay. Don't worry. I'll get you out," I said, quickly glancing around for anything that could help—a rope, tree branch, a board.

"I'll be right back," I shouted, and half ran, half skidded around the other side of the house. Peanut leapt at my feet, barking madly, loving all the excitement.

At the front of the house were several planks of wood leaning against the peeling clapboard. Frank had brought them over a few weeks earlier, ready and waiting for the first day of good weather to replace the rotting boards on Oscar's porch steps.

They were a good size—two by twelve. I heaved one up on my shoulder and slowly squelched my way back. My sneakers now looked like globs of black tar.

Oscars white eyebrows lifted at the sight of the board. "Good girl," he hollered. "Bring it here." He lifted a red arthritic hand toward me to reach for one end of the board.

I did my best to lay it flat across the mud. Peanut scampered across it, leaving muddy, pint-size paw prints.

Oscar struggled to get on the board, but it was of no use. His boots were stuck fast, from the suction, or what I couldn't tell. But he wasn't getting free.

I slowly walked out onto the board and offered him my arm. He grabbed hold of me and, with lots of grunting, managed to extricate his foot from the boot. He stepped onto the board. Then, leaning heavily on me, he pulled his other foot out. A black sock dangled from his toes. I was worried for a moment when the board did a tipsy motion, but then we were shuffling down to the end, leaving his boots behind.

With him still leaning on my arm, I walked him around to his front door. His porch was in horrible disarray, so I knew a little—or in our case a lot—of mud wouldn't make a difference, but I didn't want Peanut to run into the house.

"If you get me a towel, I'll bring her inside and bathe her really quick," I suggested.

"Bathe her? Back in my day, a dog's worth was measured by the dirt on its back. Showed it was a working dog." His words were an empty protest. He took one look at the dog, and grudgingly said, "I'll be right back."

I waited on the porch with Peanut, whistling every now and then to call her back whenever she raced off the porch. The door opened and Oscar handed me a blue-and-white striped towel, one that had definitely seen better days.

"Bear!" "Bear!" And then lower, "Confound it. Peanut!"

The little dog came running to the owner at the sound of her name, her feet a blur, like they scarcely touched the ground. I was afraid she'd bowl him over with her excitement. As little as she was, he appeared completely done in from his time struggling in the mud. I intercepted her with the towel and wrapped her up.

"Okay, show me where the bathroom is," I said.

He led me down the hallway, past his family pictures. My heart always squeezed when I saw his lovely wife. He had two boys, but I'd never seen them, and he never talked about them.

The bathroom was hideous in the way only a bachelor's bathroom can be. The tub didn't look like it had been cleaned in years.

Oscar disappeared, only to come back with a bottle of dog shampoo. "Missus bought it," he sniffed.

I turned on the water, holding the wriggling dog on my lap. "Thanks, Oscar. If you can get me a clean towel, and maybe some type of household cleaner and sponge, I'll wash the mud away when I'm done."

He mumbled something that I couldn't understand, but held the tone of a complaint. Still, he left to go track down the items I'd asked for.

When the water was warm, I plugged the tub and set the little dog in. Oscar came back with the things I'd asked for, plus a plastic cup.

"Thought it might be useful to rinse off the mongrel," he said.

I saw through his words. More than once, I'd caught the man kissing the top of Bear's head.

"Thank you. Maybe go get some clean socks and make yourself a cup of tea to warm yourself. I'll be out in just a minute."

"Tea?" he said indignantly. "It's whiskey that warms a man." Sock still dangling from one foot, he headed out, presumably to the kitchen.

I laughed and squeezed some of the dog shampoo into my hand. It had a lovely, floral scent. "You're going to be so pretty, aren't you girl?"

The happy dog panted up at me. I washed her fur and carefully untangled some burrs. Soon, she was clean and rinsed. I dried her off as best as I could and set her on the floor. She shook herself off vigorously and then raced out of the room like there was a pork chop dangled before her.

73

I held my breath, listening. A few moments later I heard a loud, "Oof! Confound it, Bear!" I chuckled as I started scrubbing the tub. She must have jumped on his lap. I made a bet with myself that she'd still be there when I was done.

Cleaning took a little longer than I expected. Once I'd finished the tub, the sink looked terrible, so I cleaned that. And then I couldn't just leave the toilet that way, so that got a scrubbing, too. Finally, I took the wet towel that I'd dried the dog with, and wiped the floor. I was really pleased with how the bathroom looked when I was finished. I washed my hands and flicked the light off with a smile.

"Where do you want me to put these towels, Oscar?" I asked, coming into the living room.

He was sitting in his easy chair with Bear on his lap. A steaming cup that looked suspiciously like tea sat next to him. But I gave him the benefit of the doubt that it also held a large helping of whiskey.

"Through the kitchen's the laundry room," he said. And then quieter, "Thank you for your help."

"You're welcome," I said.

"It pays to have a nosy neighbors sometimes," he quipped back.

I rolled my eyes, but couldn't help smiling. I chucked the stuff into the laundry room, and tried to turn a blind eye to the mess in the kitchen. One thing at a time.

Back in the living room, I asked him, "You got everything you need?"

He nodded and seemed more relaxed in his chair. I was starting to think there really was something stronger in his teacup.

"Sit down," he indicated a chair filled with magazines across from him. I hesitated, wanting to talk with the Johnson's. I'd already been gone for too long. Still, I was intrigued that he was inviting me to stay. I cleaned out the magazines and sat.

"Hard to believe I needed rescuing," he said with a sigh. "Never needed it before."

"Don't worry about it. That mud was crazy. Since you brought it up, what was it you did before you moved here?"

He laughed.

"What's so funny?" I asked.

"I was employed by the Federal Bureau of Investigation, and now I'm getting rescued from my own backyard."

My mouth dropped. I couldn't believe it. "Are you serious?"

"Yes ma'am. Official FBI agent here."

"What did you do?"

He squinted an eye at me. "You know if I tell you, I'd have to kill you."

Well, I knew he was kidding. But the expression in his eye kept me from pressing for any more details.

"Mm," he said, stroking Bear's fur. "She smells like she did when Claire was here."

"You must miss her a lot," I said, sympathetically.

"I do. I do. She was my life." His eyes got misty, and he wiped at one with a calloused hand. "Confound it," he muttered.

"I— I get it," I said. He looked over at me sharply. "I lost my fiancé a few years back. In a horrible accident." An accident that to this day I didn't understand. We'd been driving from the city, with me following him in my car. For no reason that I could understand he simply veered off the road. His car crashed through a guardrail and flipped end over end down the embankment. I swallowed hard at the memory, feeling very misty-eyed myself.

"What was his name?" Oscar asked.

I cleared my throat and tried to speak as though there wasn't a lump in there. "Derek. Derek Reynolds."

He sat up straighter in his seat. "What was his last name?"

CHAPTER 9

The intent expression on Oscar's face gave me chills for some reason. I repeated the name. "Derek Reynolds."

He sat back, his gaze tracking down to the dog. His eyebrows bunched together. Finally he said, rather anti-climatically, "I'm sorry for your loss."

Okay... what was that about? I didn't know how to respond. When it was apparent he wasn't going to say anything more, I glanced at my watch and stood to go. "You sure you have everything you need?"

"I'm fine. I'm fine," he said, waving me off. "Get out of here and take care of those guests of yours."

"All right. Good bye, Peanut," I said as I walked to the front door.

"Bear!" Oscar roared.

I smiled as I let myself out. I hated to put my shoes back on because they weren't much more than giant mud balls, but I didn't have much choice. When I looked down at my clothes as I crossed the lawn to the B&B, I realized I was a muddy mess. For a split second, I was hopeful, remembering my change of clothes from the dinner the other night. *I can at least change into clean clothes.* Then I realized I'd left them at the Miquel's manor in the chaos of the evening.

Sighing, I slipped the shoes off at the bottom of the stairs so I wouldn't track mud on the wood and let myself in. Hoping to avoid the Johnsons, I hurried to the kitchen.

"Hi GiGi. Oh my—" Cecelia's eyes widened at the sight of me. "What in the world happened to you?"

As fast as I could, I filled her in with my dealings with Oscar, and then immediately begged, "Please tell me you have something, anything, that I can change into."

"Of course, dear." Her matter-of-fact attitude snapped back into place. She led me into her room, where she pushed me toward the bathroom. "Go clean up and take a shower. I'll just have some things for you on the bed." She shut the bathroom door behind me.

I stripped off the dog hair and mud-encrusted clothes and turned on the hot water, and let out a big sigh of relief as I climbed in. The lovely water sluiced off my body, along with Cecelia's fruity scented shampoo, bringing energy back into me. Climbing out, the scent of lavender greeted me as I dried off with a fluffy towel. I held it to my nose and sniffed again. It smelled like home.

Out on the bed, Cecelia had laid out a t-shirt, a cardigan, and a pair of sweat pants. Beggars couldn't be choosers, and I was grateful for clean, warm clothes.

I didn't have a brush with me, so I ran my fingers through my short hair as best as I could, and then bunched it into a bristly ponytail.

When I returned to the kitchen, Cecelia gave me a smile of approval. "You look much better," she said as she rolled out the dough for biscuits.

"Thank you so much," I said gratefully. "Do you have anything for me to do?"

"Well, dinner is already prepared and baking. Maybe you could set the table," she suggested.

I grabbed the service basket and carried it into the dining room.

There was an open entrance between the dining room and

the living room, and I could hear the Johnsons softly talking. I laid out the silverware, the china dinner and salad plates, the cloth napkins, and then polished the wine glasses and set them in place.

Once finished, I set the basket on the sideboard and headed through the white archway into the living room. I didn't want to disturb the couple, but I was hoping they wouldn't mind some company.

The Johnsons looked up from their cards as I walked in.

"Hello, Georgie. Don't you look comfy. It's a wet day, out there, eh?" Mrs. Johnson said.

I glanced at my sweat pants and cringed. "I had to rescue a muddy dog and her owner, so Cecelia gave me a change of clothes. I am pretty comfy now, though. How are you both doing?"

"Well, my sweetheart here is kicking my rear playing Rummy," Mrs. Johnson laughed.

He snorted. "Don't let her fool ya. She just likes to lull you into a false confidence before she runs you over. She's already got five games on me at this point," Mr. Johnson said. He tossed his cards face down and stretched.

Mrs. Johnson set her cards down as well. "You ready to be

done?" she asked. When her husband nodded, she gathered the cards up and began to reshuffle.

"Look at her." Her husband admired. "Just like a card shark in Las Vegas."

His wife blushed and laughed, the cards making a soft shushing in her hands as she shuffled. "Have you heard anything more about that poor woman?" she asked.

I sat on the sofa across from them. "The last bit of news I got was that they're trying to track down what she ate."

"What she ate?" Mrs. Johnson's eyebrows drew together.

"Oh, I guess the *new* news is that she didn't choke. It turns out it was a severe allergic reaction."

"My stars!" she said, her hand flying to her chest.

"Really?" added Mr. Johnson. He shook his head in surprise.

"Yeah. But as far as I know, they haven't been able to find the allergen that she ate. There didn't seem to be anything in the menu that could have caused her reaction. It's weird. Hey, I do have a question," I hedged. Now seemed as good of a time as ever to let it fly.

"Hmm?" Mrs. Johnson smiled at me.

Word it carefully. "Err. Someone mentioned they saw you leave the table. Did you see anything of interest?"

I sat back, fully expecting her to say she went to the rest room.

Instead, she blushed. "Oh yes. I forgot my stole."

I remembered the fur stole she'd had on that night. "Where did you leave it?"

"In the drawing room. It was so warm, I'd draped it over the back of a chair." Her cheeks turned pinker. "After the glass of wine, I seemed to have gotten a little forgetful."

"Did you see anything out of the ordinary while you were in there?" I asked.

She bit her bottom lip. Her hands wrung together. "I did find something. I thought it belonged to one of the other guests so I picked it up."

"What was it?"

"It was a peacock pin. I actually have it in my room."

Mrs. Vanderton was wearing a peacock head piece. "Who did you think it belonged to?" I asked, just to see if she had the same suspicion.

"Well, I remembered Mrs. Vanderton was wearing a similar piece. I assumed it belonged to her." She frowned. "But I never did get to see her again to ask her. I'd meant to give it to Mr. Miquel, but in the commotion, I forgot about it."

I nodded. "Can I see it?"

She closed her eyes, her very being vibrating nervousness. Her eyelids fluttered, and her hands gripped the fronts of her legs. "Am I in trouble?"

"Of course not," I said. "Don't worry. But I think we should share this with the police."

She beckoned me to follow her to her room. Once there, she found her purse and, after a thorough search, she found the pin and handed it to me.

I didn't want to take the piece of jewelry into my hand just in case there was a chance of fingerprints. "Just set it on the dresser top," I said.

It was similar to the iconic peacock that I'd seen Mrs. Vanderton wearing. But it wasn't identical and appeared to be slightly smaller than the one she had in her hair.

"Good eye! Where did you find this at?" I asked.

"It was on the velvet table cloth where the saber was kept. I figured when she leaned over to look at it, maybe it just fell off?"

I took a picture of it with my phone and sent the shot to Frank. Frowning, I scrolled through our previous messages. I was a bit disappointed to see he hadn't responded to my earlier text about the cookies.

"What are you doing?" Mrs. Johnson asked. The poor woman

still appeared worried.

"I'm just letting my buddy who's on the police force know what was found. I think they'll be interested."

Frank texted back. **—What's this?**

—Mrs. Johnson found it in the drawing room. She assumed Mrs. Vanderton dropped it and picked it up to return to her.

—I'll be over to take a look at it.

I smiled as I clicked off the phone. "He's coming to get it."

"Oh, okay. Should I—?" she made as if to pick it up.

"I think we shouldn't touch it again. Just in case it helps the investigation. I've gotten into trouble for touching things in the past." I smiled at her.

"Oooh, okay," she said, giving her fingers a guilty look. "I've touched it. Did I ruin anything?"

"No. I'm sure it's fine, and I'm just being extra careful. It's Cecelia's grandson that's coming over. He's chewed me out more than once when I've touched something. His bark is worse than his bite, but I don't want to give him an opportunity to do it again."

She smiled, appearing reassured, and we headed back down to the living room.

The Johnson's had just started another game of rummy, with Cecelia bringing in a fresh fruit salad to snack on, when Frank arrived.

With the Johnson's permission, I led Frank up to their room. He studied the pin for a moment and then scooped it up into an evidence bag. Then, he tromped back down the stairs to take Mrs. Johnson's statement. When he'd finished, we headed into the kitchen.

As soon as the door shut, I turned to Frank. "So, what do you think?"

"I think it's pretty odd that it fell off her dress. You sure you saw her wearing the same peacock in her hair?"

I nodded. "Not the same, but similar. If it belonged to anyone else, I'd be shocked. They're unique pieces. Looks like an antique, actually. I wouldn't be surprised if it belonged to someone in her family."

He nodded. "All right. I guess we'll run it up to her sister and see if there's any way she can identify it."

That hardly seemed likely, given that they hadn't seen each other in years. But if it was a family piece, the sister might remember.

Little did I know it would be the coroner giving us the biggest information on the pin.

CHAPTER 10

"Hey, did you get my text about the cookies?" I asked Frank as I walked him out to his car.

"Yep. I texted you back that they were looking into it."

"You did not," I said.

"Sure I did." He started to argue, even whipping out his phone to prove it. "See," he said after scrolling a bit. "I sent it...." His voice trailed off.

"Yes?" I prompted, giving him a little nudge.

"I thought I sent it. But instead I got distracted by the file the coroner sent me." He opened the message and stared at it.

"Oh yeah? Can I see?" I leaned over his shoulder to peek.

"Get away, snoopy," he said, holding his phone higher. Really, it wasn't fair, given that he was a foot taller than my own five-foot-two.

He opened his car and gestured to the other side. "Get in. It's freezing out here."

I scrambled into the passenger side while he started the car and turned the dial to blast the heat.

"Well?" I asked, rubbing my hands together while he read the file. "What does it say?"

"I don't think this pin could have belonged to Veronica Vanderton," he said, frowning.

"That's impossible. Why not?"

He shrugged. "Well, you tell me. How many pins do you ladies wear at a time?"

"Hmm?"

"It says here in the description of the articles she was wearing that she had on one crucifix necklace, one peacock head piece, and one giant pin described here as a purple flower affixed over her heart, in addition to a watch and three rings."

"She was already wearing a pin?" I sank back into the seat feeling confused.

"Yeah. Seems like it," he sighed.

"So that makes no sense for her to have on another pin."

He pulled out the baggy and studied it. "I agree. Unless I missed something where women wear multiple pins, it seems highly unlikely that it's hers."

"This is crazy." I smiled at him.

"What?" he asked, his dark eyebrows lifting.

"If someone had told me when I was fifteen years old that I'd be sitting in a cop car with you, discussing women's pins, I'd have thought they were crazy."

"Crazy, huh? You make that sound like it's a bad thing. What's wrong with that? It's a crazy world, after all. Now, get out of here, Short Stuff, and let me get back to work." He half-grinned.

"Whatever." I got out of the car. As I turned to go, he rolled down the window.

"Hey," he yelled.

"Yeah?"

"I think I'm starting to like crazy."

I grinned as I jogged up the steps.

"Did he like the pin?" Mrs. Johnson asked as I entered. She was slipping on her coat.

"He did. I think you found a real clue," I said, giving her a thumbs up.

"Oh, good," she said, fluttering her hand to her chest. "I'm so relieved."

Her husband came down the stairs then. "You ready to go?"

"Where are you two off to?" I asked.

"We heard there's a great Amish restaurant around here. We want to check it out."

"Sunnyside Gale?" I asked.

They both nodded.

"You'll love that place. They have some banana bread that I get every time. I also recommend the apple crisp."

"Sounds lovely!" Mrs. Johnson said. Her husband held the door open for her, and they headed out.

That reminded me, I really needed to stop by there again, because it had been a while. I wonder if I could incorporate it into one of my tours.

"Is Frank here?" Cecelia called from the kitchen.

I briskly walked back there. "Yeah, he was here to pick something up, but he just left."

"That rascal. Didn't even stop to say hi to his Grandma." She was wrist-deep in dough.

"What are you making?" I asked as I started in on the dishes. Most of the pots and pans were already washed and sitting on a towel to dry. I didn't know how Cecelia did it, but she managed to cook and keep up with dishes at the same time.

"Bread for tomorrow," she said, turning it over. "What did he pick up?"

"A pin that Mrs. Johnson found at the dinner party. We thought it might be Mrs. Vandertons', but now we don't know. The coroner recorded her as already wearing a pin when she came in. Frank took it in as evidence." I finished with the wine glasses.

"I do remember her wearing a pin. A big purple one."

"I just noticed the one in her hair." Carefully, I wiped the glasses dry.

"Yes she had that one too." Cecelia flicked the dough into a loaf pan. She covered them with a clean cloth and set them by the stove to rise.

I finished drying the rest of the dishes as I thought about the other women at the dinner party, trying desperately to call to mind what jewelry they wore. Sparkling necklaces, diamond earrings, but not one came to mind that was in the antique nature.

Another thing that struck me was how old-fashioned pins were. Was it common for women to wear one at this type of dinner engagement? The last ones I'd seen was when Cecelia got ready for church. Yet, here there were apparently two women who'd worn them to an elegant dinner function.

My mind immediately went to Gayle Marshall. She *did* own that antique shop down at the centurial section of town. If I recalled correctly, there was a jewelry section. Maybe she'd worn it.

"Do you have anything else for me to do?" I asked , hopefully, as I put the last dish away.

"Sorry, GiGi." She sighed and rinsed her hands at the sink and wiped them on a towel. "I won't need you until tomorrow to help flip the place after the Johnson's check out."

We were expecting a large group of guests at four the following day But, even then, I wasn't going to be working much. They were in town for a family reunion.

I sighed. "Okay, I'll see you then."

I glanced at my watch. The Johnson's had wanted an early dinner, so it was still only five-thirty. I figured there still might be time to visit the antique shop.

The daylight was finally getting longer, and it was a relief it wasn't fully dark yet when I pulled into a stall in front of the building.

Gayle's Old Glories was adorable. It was set on the outskirts of town, with trees all behind it. The front sidewalk was crammed full of country antiques, an old milk bin, wine barrels, and a wooden table decorated to look like a potting table with flowers, a hand shovel, and clay pots. There was a rocking chair draped with an old quilt that sat near the door.

The sign in front said the business didn't close until six. I'd made it with fifteen minutes to spare. An overhead bell rang as I entered, and inside, the place smelled like every antique store I'd ever been in—old and musty.

I glanced around for Gayle. Old-time tunes played from an overhead speaker.

"Can I help you?" A woman in her forties asked from behind the counter.

I walked up to her. "Is Gayle here?"

"She's putting together a display in the back. If you wander back there, I'm sure you'll find her."

"Okay, thanks." Before I left, I examined the display counter. Underneath the glass were rows of antique costume jewelry.

Sparkles came from the paste jewels in the eyes of metal poodles, flowers, and cats.

Interesting.

Satisfied, I walked in the direction of where I heard stacking sounds. Gayle was there wearing denim capris, with her hair pinned up. She was stacking wooden fruit crates to make a display.

"Hi, Gayle. Remember me?"

She pushed back a fallen wisp and looked toward me with a smile. "No, I'm sorry, I don't think so?"

"I was one of the servers last night. At the charity dinner?"

"Oh, yes, I remember you. That was quite a night, wasn't it? That poor woman. What a shock."

"Were you acquainted with Mrs. Vanderton?"

"We'd spoken before, yes. Before last night, I hadn't seen her for at least six months. Since sometime last August."

"Well, the reason I came by was that a pin was found when we cleaned up. Someone thought it might have been yours."

"A pin?"

"Yes. A peacock broach. It looks to be quite old."

"I didn't have a broach on." She thought for a second, her eyes

94

squinting. "But you know who was wearing a peacock? Veronica Vanderton. Perhaps it fell off of her when she left the table?"

It was interesting to me that she referred to the dining room as the place it was found. Was she saying that to redirect me? But why would she do that?

"You have a very nice place here." I said, glancing around. "Have you owned it for long?"

She dipped her head in acknowledgement. "About two years. We branched out in our corporation, and I got this place for my own. I'm quite proud of it."

"I can see why. I bet it gets really busy in the summer with all the tourists."

"It does. I actually sell most of my stuff online. We have private clients." Gayle gave me a stiff smile. "I can't depend on the tourist season or the business would probably go under."

"Of course. That makes sense. Lately, I've been kind of being affected by the wan in tourists, myself. At the bed and breakfast, I mean," I added to clarify.

"Yes, Cecelia Wagner's place. Boy was Veronica mad when she lost out on it." The woman smiled, and not in a nice way.

"Yes, I heard. I guess she made some trouble for Cecelia with permits.

Gayle waved her hand. "Cecelia had nothing to worry about. Denise went to bat for her with the city permits and straightened it out."

"Denise?" I asked.

"Denise Miquel. Steve's wife." Seeing my look of surprise, Gayle continued. "Denise is one my best friends. We've been friends ever since college, where we used to compete together in a collegiate shooting program." She smiled proudly. "I'm telling you, put us together and nothing could stop us."

"You won, huh?"

"So many times. Those were the days." She looked fondly at a ring on her finger. It was a college class ring. She pointed to an engraving on the side. "See this here? That's the symbol for our shooting team."

I leaned in to look. "Wow, that's incredible!"

She nodded. "Those really were good times. Back when I felt young and invincible. Now I find treasures for others, and try not to be invisible."

"Aw, I'm sure those in your life don't feel that way. Your husband maybe?"

She surprised me by rolling her eyes. "The greatest love I've ever received was not from my husband."

I swallowed, not sure how to continue. Time to leave. "Well, I just wanted to come by and check to see if the pin belonged to you."

"No, I'm sorry. But I'll keep my ear out. We're having a city business luncheon in a few weeks. A lot of the same people will be there, so I can ask around."

"Thank you!" I said. After a small wave goodbye, I turned to go.

A city business luncheon, huh? It made sense since Gayle's husband owned half the buildings in town. But boy, that look in her eye when I mentioned the word husband. Didn't seem like there was a lot of love lost there.

As I approached the front door, something caught my attention. Hanging on the wall was a saber, complete with its leather-embellished sheath. I glanced back in her direction as a weird thought popped into my mind. *Could she have taken the sword when everyone was distracted? Maybe to sell to one of her exclusive clients?*

Okay, that's too crazy, even for me.

I dismissed that thought, completely forgetting the conversation I'd just had with Frank. It was a crazy world after all.

CHAPTER 11

*A*fter leaving Gayle's Goodies, I drove around a bit, the way I usually did when I was trying to process all the pieces of a puzzle to try to make them fit. Nothing was coming to me though, and I realized I was starving. My sweet tooth had been rearing its head lately, particularly after serving that scrumptious-looking dessert the other night. I'd been watching baking shows lately, and had a newfound confidence in my culinary skills. I could make that, right? How hard could it be? After all, I did make a chocolate cake from scratch.

I was rather proud of that one.

Plan in mind, I headed to the store. In the parking lot, I did a quick search on how to make crème brûlée. Looking at the ingredient's list, I was impressed that there were only five. Win for me, since I already had four of them at home.

I grabbed a hand basket and was hurrying toward the dairy aisle when my phone buzzed. It was Adele.

"Well, the detective just called me about those cookies." Her voice was glum. I braced myself for the news.

"Okay?"

"Apparently, the cookies were already gone by the time he stopped by today. But the butler told him that they were made fresh twice a week. Mrs. Miquel likes to have something to snack on when she visits the library."

"Did they have nuts in them?" I asked, crossing my fingers, even though Veronica didn't have a known allergy.

"Oatmeal raisin. So the investigation is back to really focusing on my menu. Police officers actually came earlier and took samples of the ingredients I brought. They even asked if I used Worcestershire sauce and anchovies."

"And nothing, right?"

"No. I already told you. I told everyone. The only seafood I had was parchment-wrapped sole, and that only went to one person."

One person ... it hadn't been on my side of the table. "Who exactly did that go to, do you know?"

"The mayor's wife."

Hmm. That didn't seem helpful.

"All right, I'll keep thinking. Don't you worry because we'll figure this out."

"I hope so, Georgie. As it is, I've had two bookings cancel already."

My heart felt heavy when I hung up. I slung a carton of heavy cream into my hand basket, grabbed some coffee and a tube of toothpaste, and headed for the check-out line.

I was on my way back out to the van when Frank texted. — **verdict is in. According to Vanderton's medical report, her only allergy was shellfish. There was nothing in there about nuts.**

So unless they had been shrimp cookies, that idea was definitely ruled out. I just couldn't wrap my mind around the question of what did she eat that had been contaminated?

The drive home was uneventful, but I groaned as I approached my apartment. Parking was completely filled in front of the building. I ended up pulling into a spot almost a block and a half away, but it was the best I could do. I hit the e-brake and grabbed my stuff, then hurried up the sidewalk.

It was dark by now, and quiet. I was turning the events over in my head, trying to figure out how else she could have eaten shellfish, when dog lunged at me from inside a parked car as I passed. I nearly dropped my groceries as I jumped, my heart beating triple time. He continued to bark as I ran up the stairs of the brick building and punched in the entry code. A buzz let me know the doors had unlocked.

I lived on the fourth floor of the building. It was a steal as far as rent went, the building was clean, and the neighbors were nice.

The door next to my apartment opened just as I reached the top of the stairs. It was Mrs. Costello. Somewhere in her fifties, she had a couple of young adult children who stopped by for dinner during the week, and she often had a plate ready for me as well. I think she felt sorry for me, but I loved it.

"Georgie! I thought it was you."

I cringed, wondering how loud I must sound thumping up the stairs for her to hear me.

"Hi, Mrs. Costello."

"I have some lasagna I just made this evening and thought you might like a slice. I was thinking you lost weight the last time I saw you. Eat! Eat!" She held out a plate.

I swear, I was the luckiest. "Thank you, Mrs. Costello."

"You're welcome, sweetie. Enjoy."

I got my key out and jiggled it in the lock until it slid it. I unlocked it and dropped my load onto the kitchen counter. Home. Instantly, I could feel myself relax. Okay, time to get the bra off, eat food, and get ready for some internet searching.

A few minutes later, first thing on the list accomplished, I settled on the couch with my laptop and the plate of lasagna. I wanted to learn a little bit more about Gayle Marshall. I typed in her business name, and Gayle's Old Glories popped right up. I took a bite of lasagna, scrolling. I wanted to see if I could figure out any of her special customers.

I searched a popular bidding site and saw quite a few things she offered. No saber, though. But if she had private clients, it wouldn't be something she advertised, anyway.

A broach resting right where the sword had once been seemed like too big of a coincidence to ignore. But I needed something more to connect her to the sword.

Frank hadn't seemed too impressed by it when I told him, but he had texted me to ask me to lunch. I was excited about that.

After about ten minutes of searching the internet, nothing else was coming up that made sense. I pushed the laptop away, feeling irritated.

All right, time to make the crème brûlée. Honestly, it sounded like fun earlier, but now that the time was here, I was feeling tired and a little unmotivated. Still, I had a goal and wanted to get it done.

I washed Mrs. Costello's plate and then got all the ingredients out and lined up on the counter.

Recipe

6 egg yolks

6 tablespoons white sugar

1 teaspoon vanilla extract

2 1/2 cups heavy cream

⅛ teaspoon salt

PREHEAT OVEN to 325 degrees

Whisk the egg yolks, salt, sugar and vanilla in a mixing bowl until the appearance is creamy.

Pour heavy cream into a saucepan and stir over low heat. Watch carefully. As soon as it comes to an almost-boil remove from heat.

Stir the cream into the egg yolk mixture until fully mixed.

Pour cream mixture into the top pan of a double boiler of

lightly boiling water. Stir continuously for about three minutes until mixture slightly coats the back of a spoon. Remove mixture from heat immediately and pour into four 6-ounce ramekins into a baking dish.

Bake for 35 to 40 minutes or until centers are barely set. The top should be slightly jiggly. Remove very carefully.

Cool in the Refrigerator for several hours and up to a couple of days. Make sure it's completely cool to withstand the heat under the broiler.

When ready to serve, sift 1 tsp of sugar on top of each custard. Place ramekins on a cookie sheet and broil 2 to 3 inches from heat source. Watch carefully. Remove when browned, approximately two minutes.

Serve within two hours.

PERFECT. I quickly blended the ingredients together. I didn't have a double boiler, but I used a trick Cecelia taught me. Three minutes later, I poured the mixture into the ramekins. Satisfied that I'd knocked this recipe out of the park, I turned the oven to broil and slid the pan in. I set the timer for forty minutes and then sat down at the kitchen table.

Resting on a tiny easel was the newest painting I'd been working on since last art class. It was of an ice-cream shop where my Grandma used to take me when I was a little girl. She always treated me to a double scoop whenever I lost a tooth. There was more than one time that I pried one out for that second scoop.

Smiling at the memory, I dipped my brush in a blue as I studied the scene again. The light in the shop window reminded me of the way the light hit the foyer floor when I'd caught Mr. Miquel pacing on the phone. "You're late! Why aren't you here?" he'd demanded to know.

Was he that upset that his wife wasn't there? He said his wife was four hours away with her mom.

Maybe I was over-thinking it too much. After all, he could have been angry with one of the help who hadn't shown up.

I thought about the argument that I'd caught Gayle in with Veronica Vanderton. Gayle had been scolding Veronica for eavesdropping, and Veronica had said she could sue her for libel. She also mentioned Gayle had stressed her out so much, she'd needed her asthma inhaler.

I frowned, wondering just what that gossip was about that Veronica supposedly had eavesdropped on. I rinsed out the brush and then hurried to my laptop. My fingers flew on the keyboard as I typed in Veronica Vanderton's name. I was curious to see what would come up.

Just like Gayle had mentioned, a court order showed up for filing chapter thirteen. Not good. After some more searching, I found something else of interest on the Gainesville's Town Gossip page. I clicked it to read.

"Blind item. What socialite is finding herself looking for a new nest? And that nest just may be with a married man."

Underneath that, someone had posted, "When life isn't happy at home, birdies often fly from the nest."

The next post was "Home? What home?"

A little cryptic. The same gossip that had been hinted at during the charity dinner. Was Valerie a kept woman? Or did this mean something else entirely different?

What was that smell? I lifted my head and breathed in. Burnt milk .... Oh no! I jumped from the couch and scrambled into the kitchen, my socks causing me to slide when I hit the vinyl flooring. I slipped on mitts and pulled the pan out of the oven.

A high pitched whine broke from my mouth. "Nooooo...." Black scorch marks covered what had once been creamy surfaces, turning the tops into lava rock.

Biting my lip, I set it on the stove top with a bang. I blew out a gust of air. What had I done wrong? I grabbed the recipe and reread it. My timer was still ticking down. In fact I had twenty minutes left on it. Was something wrong with my oven? It's supposed to be at 325 degrees. I squinted to read the temperature. Horror filled me when I realized I'd accidentally put it on broil. It was that last direction. It had stuck with me.

I stared at it with a hopeful eye. *Do I throw it out? Can I possible save it? Yes! I can save this!* I wasn't going to let lava crust stop me now.

I plucked a spoon out from the drawer and poked at it. Seemed like it might come off in one piece. Determination filled me as I scraped off the crust of one of the ramekins. *Okay, seems like it's working.* I tried not to think of it as a scab as I flipped the crust into the garbage.

What was left in the dish was black-speckled and oddly watery. Still, I took a bite.

Immediately, I spit it in the sink. That'd be a big fat nope from me. The charcoal flavor had worked its way into the scalded milk custard.

Sadly, I scraped the rest of the pans into the trash, and stacked the dishes by the sink. Then I got myself a couple of fig newtons from the cupboard. I bit into one thinking it was hardly a replacement, but it was all I had that was sweet in the house.

My phone dinged then with a text. It was from Frank.

—Just finished a high-speed pursuit of someone you met the other night.

CHAPTER 12

*I*mmediately, I replied back—**What? Who???**

I held the phone in suspense. Who was it? Minutes ticked by, and after a while, it became obvious he wasn't going to get back to me right away. I groaned, aggravated. Sure, he worked crazy hours. But how could he leave me with a text like that?

It was closer to six in the morning when he sent a text back. I'd been fast asleep and hadn't heard it ding. But it was there when I woke, saying—**Lunch later? I'll tell you all about it then.**

—**You got it.** I answered.

I got ready and headed to the Baker Street Bed and Breakfast. That morning was filled with me cleaning and flipping the place. The Johnson's had left right after breakfast, and we were due to get four couples that afternoon. It sounded like they were going to be easy guests, just in town for a family reunion. Cecelia didn't need to prepare any meals other than breakfast.

Which meant I wasn't needed either.

I was finishing a bathroom around noon when Frank texted —**See you at the park. Bring sandwiches.**

Wait. What? I laughed as I read it. That was so like him. He wanted me to bring food to a lunch he invited me to? I rolled my eyes and finished wiping the mirror, and then washed my hands.

In the kitchen, I grabbed some bread. "Cecelia? Can I make some lunch?"

She was rolling up dough for cinnamon rolls. "For heaven's sake. Can you? You mean may you."

Oops. I'd forgotten how she hated that. "Yeah, that. Do you mind if I make some sandwiches?"

"Of course not." She waved one of her hands. "Don't be silly."

"Thanks. You're the best." I grabbed the ham and condiments from the fridge. Quickly, I assembled the sandwiches, knowing he was probably already waiting for me at the park. *Serves him right for the short notice.* I decided to forgo the

110

chips in favor of a bag of carrots. I added two bottles of water, and was off for the park.

A few minutes later, I turned into Gainesville's park and chose an empty stall next to his police car. I peeked into the driver's seat but he wasn't in there. I buttoned up my jacket as I surveyed the area. *Ah, there he is.* On a bench under the trees. I grabbed the stuff and headed over there.

"Hey lady," he said, the corner of his mouth turning up ever so slightly. That was pretty much a full-fledged smile for him.

"Hi yourself. Although I feel like you owe me big time. First you leave me in suspense all night. And then you make me fix the lunch. The one you invited me to," I reminded him as I handed him a sandwich.

"Yeah, well I'm practically taking my life into my own hands right now." he said, holding up the sandwich to inspect it.

"How so?"

"Let's just say I ate your cooking as a kid. And it hasn't improved a whole lot."

I half-punched him in the arm and he laughed. Darn if his laugh wasn't worth the teasing.

"I kid. I kid," he said around a mouthful of ham. "Anyway, I come bearing some news. I figured you'd want to be one of the first to know."

111

CEECEE JAMES

"Is it about who you were chasing last night?"

"Patience, Padwan. No, this is about Adele. She's in the clear. It definitely wasn't the food."

"For real! How come?" That was great news, and I quickly unwrapped my sandwich, excited to hear what he had to say.

"The coroner determined that Veronica was murdered."

I felt the world sway under me. *No way.* "What? Are you serious?" I stared at him.

"They found a puncture mark on her leg. A forensic examination detected histamine at the site of injury."

"So, like someone stabbed her? With a hypodermic needle filled with shrimp juice?" This didn't even make sense and bordered on absurd.

"It didn't take a hypodermic needle. Her allergy was so severe that just a scratch with the allergen entering her blood stream was enough. I'm not sure how it was delivered, but the coroner said he'd seen this before with penetration of the skin from fish hooks."

I remembered her talking about her asthma. "Where was her EpiPen?"

"I didn't know that she had one."

"Yes, she said she left it in her purse. So, you're saying that when she got up from the dining table, she was fine."

"There's no evidence putting the contact with the allergen at the table. She was probably was healthy as a clam." He grimaced. "Sorry, that wasn't exactly appropriate. Anyway, the puncture the coroner found on her leg was enough to cause the fatal reaction."

"The only other person I know who left the table was Mrs. Johnson. But Mrs. Vanderton had already been gone for a few minutes by that point."

"We'll figure it out. Don't worry."

"Now tell me about last night. I almost couldn't fall asleep after that cryptic text you sent." I took a bite.

"I'm sorry. I should have thought of that. How have you been sleeping?" His eyes softened. I knew he was remembering that I no longer took sleep medicine. I'd needed it to sleep even a few hours after Derek died. It had taken me a while, but I'd finally weaned off.

"So-so. It's been kind of crazy the last few nights," I admitted.

"I'm sorry again. I'll do better next time with dumping news like that." He coughed, and I worried about his old war injury. But he didn't rub at his chest like he normally did. "So anyway, last night I was part of a chase that ended up with me doing a T-maneuver to knock the car off the road. And guess who was in the passenger seat?"

"Who?"

"Robert Evans."

"Who's that?" I had no idea.

"The kid who was the valet from the dinner. His buddy was driving the car, which was a real bummer for us because we couldn't bring Robert in. And get this. The car had just come from an area that's known for fencing stolen property."

"Are you serious? That's insane!" I finished my sandwich, wondering if Mr. Miquel had any idea whom he'd hired.

"Yeah. Even worse, he's out on bail awaiting trial. If we'd caught Robert leaving the house, we would have brought him to jail and a judge would have jerked his bail. But, as it is, the driver had no known priors and Robert said that he was an unwilling participant in the driver's car escape."

"Even though it was his car?"

"Yep. Our hands were tied. But we'll get him." Frank shoved a carrot stick in his mouth and crunched. Frowning, he lifted the bag to examine it. "Who brings carrots as a snack?"

"You don't like eating healthy?" I teased.

He crunched some more and stared at me. "I feel like I'm in grade school."

"I'll make something better tonight. You didn't give me much time."

He paused while chewing, and the corners of his eyes creased with worry.

"What?" I pushed his shoulder. "Are you serious about not liking my cooking?"

"I'm trying to remember if my health insurance is paid up." This time I got a full-fledged smile from him at my gasp. He was so darn cute. I had to glance away to keep up the appearance of being indignant. But deep inside, I was giving myself a victory lap. I was getting him to smile more and more, lately. Therefore, I won.

He went on to say, "You know I'm just kidding. Besides, I think I'm developing a taste for charcoal."

"You behave or you'll be cooking the next dinner."

"Aw, I couldn't do that to you. My cooking is even worse than yours." He wadded up his garbage and stuck it in the bag.

I stood to brush off the crumbs from my pants, and then began to pack the containers. He did the same, but he was moving so slowly I could tell he was delaying.

After the last piece of plasticware was tucked into the bag, he reached out and pulled me in for a hug goodbye. I felt him hesitate, then he leaned away a tiny bit and looked into my eyes. Slowly, he bent down and gave me a kiss.

Our first one. Soft, but not too sweet, it gave me butterflies like crazy. Good ones. The kiss was unexpected, but I was glad about that. It didn't give me a chance to overthink it.

I smiled up at him. He grinned back and stuck his hands in his pocket and glanced at the ground, like he was having an aww-shucks moment. Then he seemed to remember that he was a military veteran and cop. He puffed out his chest with a bit more machismo.

"I'll see you later then," I said, running my hand down his arm.

"Yeah. Maybe sooner than later." His aww-shucks expression was returning. I almost wondered if he was planning to kiss me again when his phone rang.

Instant mood breaker. We took a step apart, and he fished his phone from his pocket. He checked the number and grimaced.

"Sorry. I have to take this." He gently squeezed my arm, then turned to walk away. A few seconds later, I heard him answer, "Hello?"

I sighed at the abrupt end to our date, and looped the lunch bag over my arm. Thinking about the kiss, I couldn't help a tiny smile. It was a weird thing. There was a time in my life when I couldn't imagine that I would ever be able to move past Derek. But now, with Frank, moving on turned out to not be what I'd always feared—that Derek would be replaced. It was more like my heart had grown bigger to accommodate someone else. It was a good feeling.

As I walked to the van, my mind went to Robert. He'd been so cocky the night of the charity dinner, handing me back my keys with a wink. I remembered when I'd first walked outside in my search for Veronica Vanderton and had overheard a part of his phone conversation. Something about, "Don't forget, ten o'clock tonight."

I'd assumed it meant when he was getting off work, but now I wondered. Did he have something to do with Veronica's death? Had he snuck in and stole the sword when everyone was distracted by the dead body? Was that what he was doing at the fencing house?

I wiped my hand on my pants and shivered, thinking of how we'd brushed hands when he gave me the key. I'd thought Robert had ducked his head when he'd seen Frank because he'd been embarrassed to be caught winking at me. But was it because he really was a criminal? Maybe he'd been afraid Frank might recognize him.

I started up Old Bella, and waited for the usual backfire. When it didn't happen, I relaxed in the seat.

My phone buzzed with a text. Frank maybe?

I eagerly pulled it out to read a text from Cecelia. **—Can you stop at the Miquel house and pick up my crock? They'll be expecting you.**

That's right. I left my clothes there too. I started to respond when my text was interrupted by another.

From Frank, but not what I expected.

—JUST FOUND out Robert hired one of the biggest attorneys in NYC. Real curious where he got that kind of money.

—Seriously? Do you think it was from the sale of the sword?

FRANK DIDN'T ANSWER. Did Robert Evans just get away with stealing the sword? I brought up a search engine and typed in his name and scrolled through the info. His last known address was at the outskirts of Gainesville. The next link was to Gainesville police records, which said he'd been arrested five months earlier for drug trafficking charge. An undercover officer had infiltrated a smuggling ring at Bickford Bottling company. Before that he'd been a suspect in a chop-shop take-down.

Wow. Who had the Miquel's hired? Did they have any idea? Like maybe it was a good idea not to hire a criminal who likes to steal things to drive their guests cars. What were they thinking?

CHAPTER 13

I set out for the Miquel's manor right after lunchtime. The sky was overcast, making it feel much earlier in the day than it really was. Winters were long around there. Oh, how I missed the sunshine.

The entrance to the manor was even more impressive in the daylight, so I parked the van around to the side. I didn't want its ugliness to mar the picturesque beauty made by the sweeping green lawn that contrasted against the white columns of the building. Tugging the collar of my jacket up, I headed around back to the service entrance.

The manor was enormous and felt empty and lifeless as I walked around its perimeter. I half expected to see gardeners tending to the huge property, but none were working. I passed the kitchen's herb garden—which looked a little brown and run-down—and gently knocked on the lattice-covered window of the back door.

The housekeeper opened it with a smile. "Hello. How can I help you?"

"Hi, there. My Aunt Cecelia called about a crock that she left here."

"Of course. I remember you. Come in."

I followed after her, admiring how her shoes made no sound on the ceramic tile floor.

Mine, however immediately set up an annoying squeak since they were damp from my walk from the van.

"Georgie, was it?" she asked as we rounded the corner into the kitchen.

"Yes, that's right."

"We did find a few things that were left. I've had them boxed for you," the housekeeper continued. She slipped a phone from her pocket and pressed a button. When somebody answered, she said simply, "She's here."

Somehow, those words made the hair on my neck raise. She was probably just letting the kitchen staff know to bring out the box, I reasoned.

We walked into the kitchen, where a cardboard box was

indeed waiting on a giant butcher-block of a counter. I moved to grab it, when her slight cough gave me pause.

"If you could just wait here a moment," she said, with a dip of her head.

Okay...

"Mr. Miquel asked to speak with you. May I get you a cup of tea while you're waiting?"

I was about to answer when a hearty, "Ms. Tanner!" came from behind me. Mr. Miquel had been quick to come find me, it seemed. I turned to see the tanned man dressed in crisp linen pants and a white shirt partially unbuttoned.

"Hello, Mr. Miquel," I said, walking over to receive his outstretched hand. He took mine and shook it vigorously. Then, instead of releasing me, he covered it with his second hand and gave mine a warm squeeze. I stood there awkwardly, waiting to be freed.

"How are you?" he asked, his brown eyes staring deep into my own. His tone indicated we were long lost friends.

"I-I'm fine, Mr. Miquel. Just here to pick up some items left from the other night."

"Ah yes, such a shame." With one last squeeze, he let go of my hand. His eyes took on a sorrowful expression. "That poor woman."

"Were you long-time friends with her?" I asked.

"Friends." An expression passed over his face that I couldn't read. "Can you come with me a moment?" Like a magnet, he drew me out into the hall. I followed, nearly against my will.

He studied my eyes, and he sadly frowned. "The poor woman. We weren't friends. No, I was acquainted with her husband before he passed. She was invited out of respect for that relationship. Regrettably, she and my wife never got along well with one another." His eye twitched at the corner.

I nodded. He was lying to me. I could tell.

"At any rate, I wanted to speak with you. My butler informed me that Detective Kirby came by yesterday. He was asking for some information about our cookies? Apparently, the detective said that you witnessed the poor woman eating one of them?"

"The poor woman, by that do you mean Veronica Vanderton?"

"Yes, yes of course." He smiled again. It felt very fake. What was he hiding?

"No, actually it was another one of your guests. I merely mentioned it because there was some confusion as to how Veronica ingested the allergen. I'd been working with Adele, so I knew it wasn't in the food that she'd prepared."

"Oh, I see. So the police were concerned it came from the cookies. Thinking it might have been a nut allergy, perhaps?" His brow wrinkled, and he thoughtfully tapped his chin. "I believe they were raisin. My wife is very partial to them. She has a sweet tooth and loves her cup of tea and a good cookie every night while reading before bedtime."

"Yes, that's what the detective told me as well. Apparently, it's still a curiosity as to how she ingested the toxin." I hedged my story line, not wanting to reveal they'd discovered it came from a skin wound.

"I see," he said, again. He slipped his wedding ring off, and then slipped it back on. It was like a tic. I noticed something peculiar about it. "Well, if you can think of anything else that might be curious, please let my housekeeper know. I'd rather find out directly from you than the detective next time, if you don't mind. It upset my wife so. She's been in quite a state since she found out about Mrs. Vanderton. It's terribly distressing to have something like this happen in your own home, yet have absolutely no explanation."

"I can imagine so," I agreed. "And I will." I was alarmed at his need to warn me off from talking to the police.

"Well," he glanced at his watch, an expensive one encrusted with diamonds that glinted under the lights. "I need to get going. I have a golf tourney to attend."

"It was nice talking with you. Have a good game!" I said.

"It was nice to chat with you too. Take care." He turned on the heels of his white loafers and briskly walked away. I watched him pull his car keys from his pocket with a jingle, then toss them in the air and catch them. The doorman bobbed his head and opened the door. Whistling, Mr. Miquel left.

Watching him go, I realized what had been peculiar about his ring finger. When he removed the ring, the skin under it was as tan as the rest of his hand. I normally wouldn't have noticed except his skin spoke of either time spent in a tanning booth, or lots of time outside. Given that he was headed to the golf course, I guessed the later. Very curious. I brushed my hair back behind my ear and returned to the kitchen. I began to gather the box in my arms.

"Do you need help with that?" the housekeeper asked.

"No, I think I've got it."

"Why don't you go out the front door? It's quicker to your car that way."

I thanked her, and followed the direction Mr. Miquel had taken.

The doorman was still waiting by the front door. He gave me a nod as I approached.

"Have a good day, ma'am," he said and opened the door.

"Thank you." I paused, as a thought occurred to me. "Did you happen to leave the doorway the night of the dinner?

"No. I was by the door all night, ma'am," said the doorman.

"So you would have seen everyone either leaving or coming through."

"Yes, ma'am" he said, with a bob of his head.

So if they didn't leave by the front door, they must have snuck out through the back. I bit my lip, and then flashed him a smile. "I'm sorry. I just realized I forgot another one of Cecelia's pans."

He grinned and shut the door, and I hurried back the way I'd come. But instead of entering the kitchen, I exited through the rear entrance.

Standing by the herb garden, I studied the landscaped back yard. If the doorman had truly stood by the door all night, it was hard to believe someone could have left with a sword and not been noticed, no matter how distracted we all were. But he or she might have left this way.

The manicured lawn before me was painstakingly attended, dotted with bushes and trees just coming into the budding season. But, behind it all, the forest stood in the back like an impenetrable green wall.

What was on the other side of the trees? Thoughtfully, I pulled out my phone and searched for my location on a map. I zoomed out, and the picture showed the street being bordered by what looked like a large chunk of state forest. I zoomed out even more and saw a road on the other side. I stuck in a pin and then mapped directions to the road.

CHAPTER 14

With Old Bella rumbling forward, I carefully followed the map and turned on to the dirt road behind the forest. It was what appeared to be an old logging road and clearly not often used. A cloud of dust followed behind me as I drove to where I'd dropped the pin.

Finally, the phone app announced that I had arrived. The forest was so thick, there was no way to know that there were any houses in the area. Just trees as far as the eye could see. And lush undergrowth too—ferns, moss, dead branches, and rotting leaves. I parked the van and got out.

The forest was quiet, with just a breeze moving the tree tops. The van door sounded extra loud as I slammed it.

I walked to the edge of the road, the dirt crunching under my boots. Just by glancing up the shoulder, I could see that I wasn't the first one who'd been there recently. Tire tracks in the dust showed that someone else had parked there.

I didn't see any footprints indicating someone got in or out, but the dirt was scuffled from when the car had taken off. It was possible there'd been prints, but had been destroyed.

Very interesting. I pulled out my phone and snapped a few pictures of them before turning to stare into the woods. On the other side of the ditch, I thought I could make out a path where some ferns had been crushed down, a narrow one winding through the undergrowth. Was it from animals? I knew they often used the same trails.

Carefully, I climbed down into the ditch and up the bank to the other side. The forest looked formidable. I shivered as the wind blew my hair across my face. I tucked it behind my ears and zipped up my jacket. Okay, this was it.

With my shoulders back, eyes wide open for clues, I headed into the woods. The spot where I had parked was still pinned, so I wasn't too worried about getting lost. I figured I could map my way back.

I stepped carefully on the trail, looking for underbrush that had been trampled down. And it had been trampled. Not like someone leisurely hiking through the woods, but like someone had been running pell-mell out of the woods with a bear hot on their tail.

Or maybe by a bear itself.

Don'twanttomeetabear. The fear ran the thought together and repeated itself a few times before I shook my head. *Knock it off. Less imagination and more research.* I tried to orientate myself. *Okay, so the map specified that this was state forest. If I remember right, there are four manors somewhere ahead. And toward the left through the woods was the back part of town that horseshoed around.*

The clouds were breaking up, and the sun sifted through the overhead branches and brightly speckled the ground. I breathed in the scent of the wet, mulchy undergrowth, pine needles, and new sap. Even in the middle of the woods, I could smell that spring was on its way.

The path seemed like it was heading to the left, toward the estates. I followed it, carefully pushing branches out of my way. It led me deeper and deeper into the dense forest. The overhead branches wove together and smothered the sunlight.

What was that? I spun around at the snap of a branch. Holding my breath, I strained to listen. What had I done? Suddenly, the van felt very far away.

I swallowed and stared behind me. My foot slid on a branch and I reached for the tree next to me to steady myself.

Everything was so quiet.

I released my breath silently.

A gun shot rang out, and bark exploded in front of my face. I froze for a second and dropped to the ground.

I rolled to my side and wildly stared around, trying to figure out where the shot came from. My gaze caught sight of the tree I'd just been using for support. Its trunk was branded white with a fresh chew mark from where the bullet had torn the bark away.

I crawled backwards a few feet, ignoring the tree roots that my knees landed on. My heart pounded so hard I couldn't hear if anyone was coming. I felt like I was suffocating. In a panic, I stood and ran blindly.

Branches slapped my face, but I didn't feel them. My feet slipped on the muddy forest floor. I ran toward the road as fast as I could.

I cried in relief when I saw the van through the trees. I half fell, half rolled down the bank and into the ditch. My jacket pulled up, trapping my arms. I struggled to turn over, the inhibitions to my arm movement fueling my panic. Finally, I was on my feet and running for the van. I wrenched the door open with shaking hands. Once inside, I fumbled to lock it. I tried to fish my keys out of my purse and dropped them to the floor. They disappeared under the seat.

"No!" I screamed in frustration. I looked wildly about to see if anyone was coming out of the woods. Was that movement? Was that just the wind?

Leaning down, I felt around and was just able to hook the key ring on my finger. I pulled them out. Adrenaline had me shaking so hard I couldn't get the key into the ignition. I tried again. Old Bella gave her normal whirrs as she attempted to start.

"Come on, come on," I coaxed, nearly sobbing. She turned over with a cough and let out a loud backfire. As fast as I could, I turned the van around and was speeding back down the road.

I brushed my face and winced at the burn. Glancing in the rearview mirror, I saw my cheek speckled with flecks of bark and blood. My hands trembled as I pulled out my phone. I dialed Frank.

No answer.

"Frank," I left a message, trying to keep my voice light. "Hey, it's me. So, can you give me a call when you get a chance? Like as soon as possible."

I spun the wheel and turned onto the main road. My tires spat dirt, and the cardboard box holding the dishes tipped over with a clatter. I didn't care. I just wanted to get out of there and home as fast as I could.

Calm down. Breathe. Who just shot at me? How did anyone know I was there? Had someone followed me into the woods? But how could they have known where I was going? That's impossible.

The more I thought about it, the more outrageous it seemed that this had been done deliberately. How could anyone have guessed that I'd be in the woods today? And who out there would want to wish me harm?

By the time I pulled onto Baker Street and rattled down the gravel road to the bed-and-breakfast, my body was calming down. Another thought occurred to me, making me feel ridiculous.

You idiot, you went tromping out into the woods during hunting season, I bet. You didn't even check.

I parked the car in the driveway and did a quick search on my phone.

February hunting season.

I scrolled until I hit the Pennsylvania guide lines. I couldn't help a small frown. It didn't bring up what I was expecting. No deer or bear. So far, the seasons that came up with were for raccoons, coyotes, fox, and bobcats. I put the phone away feeling puzzled. People *did* hunt those. I guess it was possible.

My phone rang. Frank.

"Yeah?" he said, always effervescent with charm.

"Frank. I just got shot at. With a gun."

There was silence. I looked at the phone to make sure we hadn't been disconnected.

"Are you okay?" His voice sounded like he was being strangled.

"Yes. I'm fine. I'm sitting outside your grandma's right now."

I wish I could say he handled it calmly. But what came out next was a torrent of exclamations that I couldn't make head nor tail out of.

"Frank. Calm down. I can't even understand you."

I heard him do some deep breathing. And then, "Georgie, how did this happen? I've been with the force for several years, and I've only been shot at a few times! Where were you?"

I explained the dirt road where I'd been and then rather reluctantly admitted that the forest may have been zoned for hunting.

He grunted. "I don't know about that. The only kind of hunting allowed in that area would be with a shot gun," he said. "Was it a shot gun blast?"

"I don't know. It was loud."

"Tell me exactly where it was," he said. "We might still be able to track down the shooter."

I glanced at the pin on the map. "I'm not sure I can. It's kind of in the middle of nowhere, but I can lead you there. I have it on my map. I'll meet you at the entrance to the forest service road."

I held my breath, not sure how he was going to receive that. It sounded like a growl, but he said okay.

I felt a million times better knowing he was involved. He'd track down the answers, I was sure of it. Fingers crossed.

CHAPTER 15

Frank met me at the entrance and followed me down the logging road. I saw another cop car coming toward us from the other way. It spun around and followed us as well.

I led them to where I'd dropped the pin on the map and parked the van. I climbed out just as Frank and the other officer slammed their car doors. The two men walked over to where I was standing.

"So, it was up there," I said, pointing to where the ferns were smashed even further by my scramble to escape earlier.

Frank stared at it and his forehead puckered. His jaw moved like he was clenching his teeth. Finally, he ground out, "Why on God's green earth were you bushwhacking through the woods, Georgie? Obviously, it was spur of the moment."

"How could you tell?" I asked.

He glanced at my clothing attire. "No boots. Pants have grass stains, and they look like work pants."

I glanced down and groaned. I didn't have money for new ones. "I was curious if that's how the person left the manor with the sword."

"You were curious...." His voice trailed off as his hand came to rub his temple. "Never mind. Of course you were." He sighed and then gave me a look of surrender. "And what did you discover?"

"Well," I bit my lip. "I discovered that path."

"That path right there?" he pointed to where the other officer had already crossed the ditch and was examining.

I nodded.

"The one that you obliterated?"

I groaned. "Frank, I swear I didn't know that it could have been evidence, or I never would have checked it out. It just seemed like a hunch, so I thought I'd just take a peek."

"Well, come on, Miss Peeker. Lead the way." He made a

dramatic gesture with his hand. I glumly tromped back through the ditch and up the other side.

Why did it always work out this way? What was I supposed to do? Call the police and say, hey, do you think the bad guy could have gone through the woods? I'd be calling them all the time. Wouldn't anyone have driven around to check?

After a few false starts, I was finally able to find my way back to the tree. Frank followed, murmuring to the officer behind him. I recognized his partner as Officer Jefferson, one Frank had worked with before.

"There it is, right there." I pointed.

Frank's face creased with worry as he examined the tree.

"Did you bring the metal detector?" he asked Officer Jefferson.

"Yeah, I'll go grab it."

Officer Jefferson headed back to the vehicles, while Frank bent down to study the white gash in the bark.

"Yeah, this doesn't look like a shot gun," he murmured, more to himself than to me.

"So it wasn't a hunting discharge then? Since you can only legally hunt with a shotgun in this area?" I asked.

"I don't know whether or not it was a hunter for sure. Oddly enough, not everyone follows the law. I call it job security."

His response made me relax. Frank was back to his sarcastic self. I figured that meant he wasn't mad at me anymore.

Jefferson came back with a metal detector. He turned it on and it squawked and beeped a few times. When it had settled down, he began walking in lines, swinging it slowly from side to side.

"Jefferson will find something. We need the bullet so we know exactly what type of rifle or pistol was used." Frank fished out a pen light and began to examine the bullet mark. After a moment, he opened a knife and gently pried up the bark.

I stood there watching them work. Jefferson searched for about an hour, traveling up and down in an attempt to determine the direction the bullet may have ricocheted after it hit the tree. Frank took several measurements trying to resolve which way the bullet had come from. Neither man was having any luck.

The sun was starting to set, cloaking the forest in a dark gloom. I shivered and zipped my jacket higher. With Frank's permission, I'd started to search myself, scuffling through piles of leaves and fallen debris. It was a big forest and it totally felt like searching for a needle in a haystack.

"Well, boss," Officer Jefferson said with a sigh. "I'm not getting so much as a blip."

Frank shook his head. I knew how stubborn he was, and how much it bothered him to not be able to find the bullet.

"Unbelievable," he growled. He stared at me, his hazel eyes sparkling intensely. His expression alarmed me at first, until I realized the emotion he was showing was fear. "Georgie, that was too close. You could have been killed. You should know better than to come out in the middle of the woods without wearing orange."

"I had no idea...." I began.

He cut me off. "Do you realize that if you'd been hit, there would have been no help coming? It would have just been you, alone out here in the cold and darkness. Even if the bullet hadn't killed you, hypothermia would have. Or wild animals that would have only seen wounded, helpless prey. It would have been *days* before anyone happened back on this road and found your van."

"I'm sorry. I didn't mean to do anything wrong," I said, a little defensive. "I was just checking out a hunch. You can't be bothering the police with every little thing, you know."

"No, but you could have let someone know where you were going. Especially when it's a place as remote as this."

Hey, now. I was used to being independent, and so was he. I opened my mouth to protest when it occurred to me that he was wanting to be that person for me.

"Okay, sorry," I said, wanting to leave it alone for now.

He grumped some more, his hands jammed into his pockets. Officer Jefferson watched him, looking like he was waiting for the word that he could take off.

"I need to get going," I told Frank. "Your grandma has a full house tonight. I should have been there already to help out."

He nodded brusquely, still looking frustrated. "Fine. Go. I'll catch you later."

I made my way out of the woods, leaving the two of them there. The sun had dipped below the horizon when I reached the ditch. I slid down the bank and tromped back up to the road.

Back at the B&B, I sat in the van for a moment. Curious, I brought up the map of the woods. Was it just a hunter? I zoomed out from the pin. My eyebrows lifted when I saw that another road ran parallel to the dirt one I'd been on.

I zoomed out some more.

It was the same road that Gayle's Old Glories antique business was on. Did someone take the sword to her place? Or, was that some kind of coincidence?

CHAPTER 16

Mornings were never my favorite time. But over the last few months, I'd been making more of an effort to have a good attitude. Every new day really was a gift, I reasoned. Derek would have loved to have had a chance to wake up today.

I'd even gotten a new alarm clock. It was the coolest thing. About ten minutes before it was time to wake up, it would softly glow. The light would grow brighter and brighter to mimic the rising of the sun. All I know is that even through my closed eyelids, I could "see" it. And by the time the alarm went off, I was already half-way awake and ready to start my day.

But this morning, it was the ringing of my phone that woke me, long before any light started on my alarm clock. I rolled to my side and grabbed it, still only able to open one eye. The person hung up while I was still fumbling to hold the phone right side up and find the button to answer it. I let out a groan and squinted to read who had called.

The number was unknown, and the person hadn't left a message.

An unknown number. That was the worst. I couldn't even search the number to figure out who it was.

I glanced at the time—a quarter to six—and rolled to my back. I had to get up. I didn't trust myself to stay in bed. I'd probably fall asleep again, and no amount of alarm would wake me this time.

I sat up with a groan, noticing with a grimace that I seemed to be doing that more often these days. I stood with a groan, got out of the van with a groan, stooped to tie my shoes with a groan. Before I could think too deeply about what that meant, I stumbled for the shower.

Showers always broke the morning blues. Hot water, my strawberry-peach gel, and a new razor. Heaven was a new razor and shaving cream, I swear.

Feeling much more alive after the shower, I dried my hair with a towel as I headed for the kitchen.

"Momma needs a cup of coffee," I mumbled, filling the

reservoir with water. The rich scent of the coffee grounds made me smile as I put in a couple scoops.

The machine made happy burps and gurgles as I sat down at the table. Resting on the easel was my newest painting. Last night, I'd finished the one of the ice-cream shop and started this one, a simple stand of saplings with the sun trickling through their baby leaves. It reminded me of my childhood.

Honestly, most of my paintings were of childhood. It had been such a happy time in my life, where my biggest worry wasn't about how I was going to pay rent, but if I could find someone's lawn to mow so I could get a new tube for my bike tire. It really made me sad when I heard other people didn't have such great memories of their own childhoods.

Frank had been my buddy back then. There'd been a group of us kids that used to hang out, and he'd been the tall, serious one. I used to love to tease him, taking it as a personal challenge to try to get him to crack a smile.

Not a lot had changed since then, I thought wryly.

As I studied the painting, it reminded me of how we used to play Robin Hood as kids. We'd cobble together these ridiculous bows and shoot homemade arrows at targets. The bows rarely worked, often causing the arrows to go in crazy directions, sometimes landing straight in the ground a few feet from where we stood.

Frank always accused me of doing that to him on purpose. Smirking, I'd sworn up and down it was an accident.

I really had been a brat.

Anyway, I remembered when Frank—who'd always been the richest kid among us, having saved his money like a ten-year-old scrooge—bought a sling shot.

Target practice changed for us from that day forward. If Frank was in a good mood, he'd let us each take a turn at the target. We'd shoot pinecones, rocks, even ball bearings and marbles from that slingshot.

And what was Frank's payment to use his slingshot? We had to go find the used ammunition among the forest floor. I'd search and find my eight marbles and he'd let me have a few more turns again.

Those marbles went everywhere, I remembered. But I got pretty good at guessing where they'd land.

That memory churned in my mind all morning as I helped Cecelia. It was another dreary day, and rain pounded against the roof. But we had a fire crackling in the living room, and Cecelia had made fresh cinnamon rolls, filling the house with a cozy, sugary smell.

The guest's family reunion was over and they checked out soon after breakfast. It was going to be another long day of flipping the bed-and-breakfast. There were no new guests scheduled until the weekend, which eased the pressure that I needed to work fast, but increased my stress about where the money was going to come from to pay the bills.

I shook the sheet onto the bed and tucked it in. *I'm not going to worry about that now. I'll think about it tomorrow.* Ever since I'd seen Gone with the Wind as a teenager, I'd adopted Scarlett O'Hara's attitude about worry for my own.

At about two p.m., we had the B&B in relatively good condition in preparation for the new guests, so Cecelia told me that I could go home. Specifically, she'd said, "Get out of here and don't get into any more trouble," while pressing a container of leftovers into my hand. Of course, I took the food, but I wondered what kind of trouble she meant. Did Frank rat me out? Again?

Before I went home, I made a stop at the local drug store. *I'm not getting into any trouble. Just going to pick up a little toy.* I was disappointed to see they didn't seem to make toy sling shots anymore. That and good old lawn darts, gone with my childhood. I did buy a bag of marbles and then headed across the street to the sporting goods store.

There, I found a slingshot as well as an orange beanie. I had a little nerve-wracking moment while trying the beanie on. I was, figuratively speaking, putting all my eggs into one basket that the shot fired in the woods had come from a hunter. With that in mind, hopefully, the hat would do its job of alerting hunters that I was human, because it could just as easily become a neon target.

It was about three o'clock by the time I drove out to the logging road to the spot I'd pinned in my maps the day before. I'm not going to lie, my hands were sweating and my heart pounding a little.

Just before I climbed out, I texted Frank. —**Hey- just doing my part to let you know I'm checking something out in the woods again. Talk to you soon.**

Then I put the phone on silent because I didn't want to listen to his "yell texts" back at me.

With a pocket full of marbles, the orange hat on my head, and slingshot in hand, I climbed down the slope and up the other side of the ditch. I followed the trail back to the tree that had been damaged by the bullet.

It was cold and wet from the rainstorm earlier. Water droplets fell around me from the overhead branches. The gash stood out white against the dark wet trunk. My skin crawled and my senses warned me to get out of there. I scanned the trees and underbrush but didn't see anything. I studied the mark again, just in case there was something I'd missed before, but all I saw were drips of sap as the tree began to heal itself.

147

A big water droplet fell directly between my eyes. I wiped it off with the back of my hand, then carefully took about fifteen steps away from the tree in the direction I thought the bullet might have come from. My fingers were wet and cold as I fumbled to get a marble out of my pocket. Tongue sticking out, I loaded the leather pocket of the slingshot, took aim, and let it go.

It flew right past the tree. I rolled my eyes and sighed. Apparently, my marble slingshot skills had deteriorated through the years. I stretched my shoulders, loaded up with another, and took aim again. This time, a little lower and to the right.

TWACK! I smiled with satisfaction at the sound. I'd seen which direction the marble had bounced off to and headed for it. I found it sitting under a pile of dead leaves. Leaving the marble where it was, I scanned the forest floor, moving slowly in an expanding circle.

I was looking for anything metallic or shiny, but nothing popped up.

After ten or so minutes of searching, I gave up and went back to the tree. This time I took fifteen steps slightly to the left. Taking aim, I shot the marble again.

Smack! The marble ricocheted to the right. I did the same

circular search as before. I was frustrated to get the same results.

Six marbles later, and I was ready to pull my hair out. I was second guessing everything, even the stupid itchy hat. I'd forgotten to be scared of who might be in the woods. All that was on my mind was finding that bullet. *It's got to be around here somewhere. What am I doing wrong? Or is this a crazy test, anyway?*

Think smarter. Don't let frustration do the thinking for you. I took a deep breath and pulled up the map, trying to rally. I placed a pin at exactly where the tree was, and then zoomed out so I could locate the second pin. Moving to the left, I tried to line myself up with both of the pins.

As if the two pins made a straight line, I continued the line deeper into the woods away from the tree. About fifteen feet away, I let another marble fly.

This time the marble nicked the tree and flew to the left. My heart pounded with excitement as I hurried to find it.

"Come on, come on," I muttered. The undergrowth seemed to have matted itself together for the sole purpose of making it hard to see under. I found it and started my circle, checking under rocks and twigs. My third circle around brought me close to the road, about twenty feet from the place where I'd entered the forest.

I walked out to the top of the bank and stared down. Was it possible? I scrambled into the ditch and checked around. At the bottom, I noticed the dirt seemed to have been disturbed. I squatted and began to sift through it with my fingers.

My heart leapt into my throat. There it was. Intact and shiny.

The bullet.

CHAPTER 17

*O*h, *my gosh! Oh, my gosh! I found it!* Excitement zinged through my body like a shrill whistle, and I covered my mouth to smother uncontrollable giggles.

Who would have thought that I could have—?

My phone vibrated, cutting off my thoughts. I pulled it out and saw an alert for a voice mail. I'd forgotten I'd turned it to silent mode earlier and hadn't heard it ring. The number was again unlisted. Frowning, I pushed play on the message.

There was just a long silence.

And then the sharp crack of a gunshot.

I jerked and dropped to the ground. *What was that? I've got to get out of here. But I can't leave my bullet.*

It had been a recording. I hadn't heard anything in the woods, so there was no reason to think he was here now. Hands shaking, I found the camera mode and took a picture of the bullet.

Then, creeping along the ditch back to the van, I called Frank.

"Georgie?"

"I didn't think you would answer." My nerves were shot. Tears stung my eyes at the sound of his voice.

"I'm almost there." He growled. "I can't believe you went back out to the woods. You're giving me gray hair, woman. I'm really going to get you back for this."

"Don't even joke," I said. "Someone just left a message on my phone. Frank... it was a gun shot."

Cursing broke out on the other end of the phone, so loud I had to hold the receiver from my ear. "What are you trying to do to me?" he finally sputtered. I could tell he flipped the siren on because I heard it through the phone. Seconds later, I heard the sound coming up the road. He was close.

"Get down," he said. "Take cover behind a tree."

"I'm in the ditch by the van," I whispered. The siren grew louder and then he was there. I heard his car door slam shut, and that was it.

Where is he? I straightened a bit to peek over the ditch's edge. His car was there, but he was missing. I turned toward the woods, trying to listen, straining to see through the trees. No noise, no movement. A lump grew in my throat.

"Frank?" I called. I crept toward my van. After checking one final time into the trees, I darted out and around the front of the vehicle.

"I'm right here," he said from the driver's side.

I practically ran into him and let out a frightened squeal. "What the heck are you doing?"

"I was doing some surveillance," he muttered. He stared at the slingshot in my hand and raised an eyebrow. "I don't even want to know what you were doing. Now let's get out of here."

"Wait," I said. "You're not going to believe it. I have to show you what I found."

He stared back at me, not with his normal expression of impatience, but one of fear. His lips tightened, and then he gave a stiff nod.

"I found the bullet," I said, this time feeling excited. Staying stooped over, I led him to the spot.

"Stooping over is just going to give them a lower target with that orange hat on your head," he noted.

I pulled it off, and then didn't know where to put it. Finally, I stuffed it down my shirt to hide it.

Frank wasn't paying attention. He'd found the spot I'd cleared and was bending down to the bullet. He whistled in amazement as he pulled out a knife and carefully pried it out of the dirt. With a plastic baggy, he scooped it up.

He stood, flashing me a smile. "You are amazing. Now let's get out of here."

We hurried to the van, with me fiercely whispering all about my bullet-finding techniques. He nodded the entire time. Before I finished my story, he opened the driver's door.

"Just get in. We'll talk about this later."

"Where are we going?" I asked.

"Your place," he said.

I climbed in and he shut the door behind me. I watched him walk to his car. The entire time he stared warily into the woods.

He followed me to my apartment and trekked up the four stories to my floor. The hallway smelled of old onions from one of my neighbor's dinner the night before. I unlocked the door and we went inside.

He sank down in the kitchen chair like he was feeling old. I flipped the phone onto speaker mode and slid it across the table toward him. He stared at the triangle and then hit *play* on the message.

"Well?" I asked, when it was finished. "What do you think?"

"I think the sound matches the bullet you found. Sounded like a high-powered rifle." He lifted the baggy and shook it slightly, eyeing the bullet. "I can't believe you found this. One in a million, I know exactly what kind of rifle shot it."

"You can? How?" I leaned to look closer.

He licked the corner of his lip as he held the baggy up to get more light. "You see how little damage is on it?"

I nodded.

"That's because it's 32 Winchester Special. They're made to not break apart and mushroom on impact. And, unlike a 30-30, a 32 caliber not common. This came from a Winchester Special model 94 rifle. I'll get forensics on it right away."

"There was something else," I thought, remembering. I scrolled to my pictures and found the one with the tire tracks. "I'm sorry. I forgot to tell you about it after I got shot at."

He zoomed in on the picture and then sent me a wry look.

"I'm sorry." I shrugged.

155

With a sigh, he forwarded the picture to his phone, which gave a ding as it received it. Then, he studied it again.

"Tire tracks look sporty." He zoomed in some more. "But, I think I see some siping on them."

"Siping?" I asked. I thought about it. "Oh, is that when they make little cuts in your tire to help grip during rain storms?"

"Yeah, that's exactly it."

"It seems unusual they aren't snow tires."

"Some people chose to do this instead, especially for a car they aren't driving in the snow." He zoomed in on the side of the track. "And the track mark is firm. These look like fairly new tires."

"New, or on a car not driven very often."

"Exactly." He shut the screen and pushed the phone in my direction. My painting on the table caught his attention.

"Nice. That's the empty lot by the old hardware store?"

"Yeah." I smiled.

"I remember that. Before the Marshall's bought it."

"That's right. I'd forgotten that. Gayle and her husband then sold it to a developer who made the business complex."

He hummed in agreement glancing around the kitchen. "Yep.

Well I have to get back to my shift." His gaze stopped cold. "What on earth is that? You trying to make diamonds?"

I turned to follow his look. The stacked ramekins by the sink and betrayed me. "Ha. Ha. Very funny. I'm super bummed they didn't turn out as expected." I walked over and sadly scraped at the crusty brûlée remnants with my fingernail.

"It's what I expected." His face was so serious that I gasped, and then he relaxed into a small grin.

I swatted at him with the dish towel. "Oh my gosh! What's gotten into you? You're cracking jokes off left and right nowadays. I guess you'll be quitting your day job and taking your act out onto the road." I set the dish into the sink. "Of course, you'll starve."

He chuckled softly and then stood up and stretched. "That's one thing I've always admired about you, Georgie."

"Admired about me? Do tell." I was all about hearing admiration.

"You're smart, you're determined, and you don't quit. I fully expect you'll be opening your own bakery before the year's out." He wrapped me in his arms. "And I'll be your best customer."

"Seriously?"

He spent the next few minutes showing me how serious he was. I had a big smile on my face when I told him goodnight.

That bit of joy stayed with me as I made some dinner and then settled down for a spree of baking shows. I *could* do it, couldn't I?

Right around eleven, as I was brushing my teeth, the phone rang. I spit out the toothpaste and ran for it.

Unlisted number.

I clicked the button, feeling nervous. "Hello?"

No answer.

I hung up and immediately dialed Frank. "He's called back!" I said, trying to sound brave and not at all like I was freaking out like a chicken laying her first egg.

He went straight to the point. "Who's your phone carrier?"

I let him know.

"Okay, I'm on it," he said. "Don't answer it again."

"All right, I won't. And there's one more thing. Mr. Miquel told me that if I thought of anything else, for me to go to him, and not the police. He was not happy about the cookie."

"Not happy about us asking about the cookie?"

"No. I guess the detective showing up upset both Mr. Miquel and his wife."

"All right. Noted. Don't worry about the phone calls. I'll get him." he said to reassure me, and then hung up.

I finished brushing my teeth and cleaning my face, and then went to bed. It was a very uneasy night's rest.

CHAPTER 18

The next morning I woke to a text from Frank. —**I
pulled some strings. The calls have
been made at the four hundred block, down by
the Jack Knife. It's a bar.**

I sat up in bed and thought about that. I knew what it was,
although I'd never been there before. But something wasn't
adding up. My first phone call came before six am. The bar
closed long before that. How could the calls have come from
the bar?

With Cecelia not needing me, I spent the day doing some
chores. I changed the bed, cleaned the bathrooms, and spent
an hour saving the ramekins.

The rest of the day was spent folding clean laundry in front

CRÈME BRÛLÉE TO SLAY

of my cooking shows. They inspired me once again, and it was about seven-thirty that night when I decided to head down to the store to get some more cream. I had to try to make the crème brûlée again. I couldn't let it conquer me.

But first, I wanted to figure out who exactly owned the Jack Knife. I typed the name of the bar in the search box. GreenLeaf Incorporated was the name that came up. I frowned in surprise. I'd never heard of it before, and I honestly thought it would have belonged to the Marshall's company.

I searched up GreenLeaf. The only other thing that came up under that name was a shipping company by the name of Bickford Enterprises in the next town over. A huge drug bust went down there about five months earlier. I closed the laptop, more puzzled than ever.

On my way to the store, I saw the Jack Knife's sign up in the distance. My curiosity was building, and by the time I came back out of the store with my cream, I'd made up my mind.

It was still early yet. The hardcore crowd didn't even start until nine or ten, at least in the movies. Didn't seem like there could possibly be anything that could go wrong.

I drove to the bar and walked in. Wow, it had been a long time since I'd gone to a bar alone.

It was dark inside, with fly-trap strips hanging from the

ceiling. I eyed them suspiciously. It being winter, I hadn't seen too many flies. I didn't know if this meant the strips were never changed, or this place was maggot infested.

A sharp *crack* drew my gaze to the far corner where a pool game was going on. Several men in jeans and torn t-shirts laughed at whomever had just made the last shot. Their laughter was loud and raucous.

I glanced at the bar. The stools were half-filled with customers who looked like they called that place home.

I didn't know what I was looking for. What was I thinking? That I'd find someone sitting in a dimly-lit corner booth, wearing a shirt with the word "Killer" on it? I must have been nuts.

Just as I was chiding myself for acting like this was some TV show, I saw him. And he *was* sitting in a booth in a dark corner.

With wild hair and a grizzly beard, he squinted at me suspiciously. I felt a chill run up my neck, and I hurried to look away, but not before I caught his sneer as he took a long drink from his beer.

I walked over to the bartender, who wiped the bar with a rag that looked like it'd been used to clean the floor. After eyeing the floor, I realized that'd probably never happened.

"Hey," I said, resting my fingers on the counter. I quickly removed them. The counter was greasy and covered in crumbs.

"What would you like?" he asked with a bored expression.

Something hard, I figured. Look like I know what I'm doing. I remembered what the attorney I used to work for always ordered. "A highball?"

He rolled his eyes, and I thought he was going to say something, but instead he pulled out a glass and mixed the drink. *Wow. That's a lot of whiskey. And just that tiny splash of soda? Okay, then.*

He slid the drink toward me and went to help the customers at the other end. Fingerprint marks marred the outside of the glass. I set a ten on the counter and took a small sip. *Whoa.* Feeling like flames were flying out my nose, I tried to look casual as I glanced down the bar.

Three phone calls had come from here. Each one at a different time. And at least two had come when the bar wasn't open. How was that possible?

A few minutes later, the bartender moseyed back my way. He set down a bowl of peanuts and his meaty hands gripped the edge of the bar. "Now what will you really be having?"

"How'd you know I wouldn't like this?" I asked.

163

"I've been doing this for thirty years. You don't belong in a place like this."

The group of men playing pool shouted, causing me to jump, underscoring what the bartender was saying.

"I just have a question," I said.

He pulled a terry cloth rag from his apron pocket and wiped his hands. "Of course you do. Let me guess. You want to know if I'd seen a man in here with a girl. Your husband?"

I shook my head. "No—"

"Boyfriend then. Lady, if you're worrying about him, you're probably right. Drop him." His eyes dipped to take in my chest. "A woman like you could have your choice of men." He smiled at me then, revealing a gold cap on one of his eye teeth.

I repressed a shiver. "No, actually I keep getting phone calls from here."

"Phone calls?" His crazy eyebrows lifted in disbelief. "Only phone we have here is in the back. Trust me, no one's been using it." He glanced out at the crowd. "Half these guys wouldn't know what to do with a cell phone. Must be some weird fluke. Sorry, lady. I think your luck's run out."

"Okay." I reached for a peanut, stopping as soon as my fingers touched the bowl. Who knows how many other hands had dipped into there. I pulled away, resisting the urge to wipe my hand on my pants. The bartender started to drift away.

"Hey, just one more thing!"

He turned back with a bored expression.

"Is there an apartment or something upstairs?"

He came back and his brows lowered. "You know, lady, I don't normally answer questions for free."

"Oh. Of course." I reached into my purse, hoping I had more cash on me. Ahh, there it was, my emergency ten. I pulled out the wrinkled bill and smoothed it out on the bar. With a smile, I slid it over.

He shot it a look of disgust. "Seriously, lady?" With a roll of his eyes he pocketed it. "There's a locked room upstairs. Sometimes the owners use it, but usually it's empty. Now, I suggest you beat it." He glanced at the pool table. "Because those boys over there are thinking you're starting to look a mite interesting."

I followed his gaze and felt my blood run cold. The men were indeed staring at me with leers on their face. *Okay, then.*

"Thank you for your help," I said and stood to go.

A hard hand clapped onto my shoulder from somebody

behind me. I squealed and spun around, ready to give someone a poke in the eye.

Frank stood there, his lips thin and pressed together. He was still in his police garb. The chatter in the bar quieted.

"How in the world?" I was shocked.

"I was driving by and saw your car. What are you doing here?"

"Uhh…" I didn't know how to answer.

"Well, now you found her. Can I suggest you take her and both go?" the bartender said. Frank narrowed his eyes, and the bartender raised his hands and backed away.

"Come on," Frank said between clenched teeth. "Let's get out of here."

We headed out and Frank walked me to my van.

"Honestly, I was fine," I said.

"You *looked* fine. Cozy even." He opened my door and then crossed his arms.

I took a deep breath. Time to address this. "Listen, I get that you worry about me. But you need to realize I'm a grown woman, not the same teenaged kid you used to hang out with. I'm independent and have been doing stuff like this"—I motioned to the bar behind me—"all of my life. I'm fine, really."

His gaze flicked to the door where two men busted through to the outside. They squared off as if about to deck each other. Frank gave a whistle, and they glanced over. They took in his uniform, and each got on their bikes and took off.

He lifted an eyebrow. "So, you were saying? All of your life?"

I rubbed the back of my neck. "Well, there was a bit more dancing at the ones I went to."

Another man stumbled out. He wore greasy overalls and old boots. We watched as he wandered down the side of the building, pausing at the corner to throw up. I grimaced, but then stood up straighter. Because what he'd thrown up against was a pay phone.

What? A phone booth? We still have those in this day and age?

"Frank," I said. "I think I know how all the phone calls were made from here."

He noticed it too, and then turned and studied across the street. "I doubt any of those places have security cameras trained this way. But I'll search into it tomorrow. And you might be all big and tough and independent, but don't forget the last few times I've found you, you've either been shot at, or about to get jumped in a bar. So don't make me sound like some over-protective twit over here."

"Okay. How about just a regular twit?" I gently teased him, hoping to get him out of his bad mood.

It didn't work. He lowered his brows, and I quickly held up my hands. "I'm kidding. I'm kidding." I said. "I'll see you tomorrow, all right?" I climbed into the driver's seat.

"Tomorrow then. And stay out of trouble." He shut the door behind me.

Wow, I must have really made him mad. I sighed and turned on my blinker. I'd think about it later. Right now, I needed to get home and do my own searching.

CHAPTER 19

*I*nstead of doing anything productive, I went straight to bed. I had to be at the B&B early the next morning and I was wiped out.

I arrived after breakfast to take the guests on a tour of several Amish markets in the Gainesville area. Cecelia had a luncheon planned, so I had them back by noon. Lunch wasn't quite ready, so, after a quick handwashing, I got to work preparing a salad.

The front door slammed, and a few moments later Frank poked his head into the kitchen.

"Hey guys. Am I in time for some food?" he asked, his eyebrows raised in question.

"You're in time to set the table," Cecelia quipped, nodding

her white head toward the serving basket. Her perfect bun didn't so much as wiggle.

Frank rolled his eyes, but wandered to the sink to wash his hands. I smiled as I continued to chop lettuce.

"What's so funny, chuckles?" he muttered, catching my grin.

"Nothing delights me more than to see you do some of your favorite chores." I remembered how he'd used every excuse possible as a kid to get out of setting the table. The only thing worse than that for him was washing dishes. "Do you have a cutlery phobia that I should be aware of?"

"I don't get why we don't just use plastic silverware and paper plates." He jerked up the basket, causing the silverware to jangle against each other and the plates to rattle.

"You be careful with that, young man. And come here and give your grandma a kiss."

He walked over and kissed her wrinkled cheek. Then he stomped into the living room, clutching the basket in his oversized hands.

I heard the plates banging on the table and snickered again.

"That boy, I swear," Cecelia whispered, a dishcloth in her hands. She used it to pull a casserole from the oven and set it on the stovetop. The scent of garlic parmesan filled the air.

"Good grief, what's that? I'm drooling," I said.

"Creamy garlic-parmesan chicken wings. They asked for finger food." She fished out another dish, this one with rolls, and set it down next to the first with a clank. "And these are ham and cheese sliders. Now, how's the salad looking?"

"Good," I said. I reached into the freezer where Cecelia's glass salad bowl had been chilling. Quickly, I assembled the hearts of romaine, radish, cucumbers, carrots, and sliced cherry tomatoes. Then I retrieved the carafes of fresh ranch, olive oil, and wine vinegar.

"Just going to take these out to the tables now." My hands were full.

"Good. And would you set out extra napkins? And the water pitchers with lemon?"

"You got it." I brought the salad out to the table where Frank was sullenly rolling the linen napkins.

"Get a move on it," I said. "Keep those napkin edges together. It's got to look classy."

"Oh, like you'd know classy. Apparently, you measure it by how many bowls of peanuts are on the bar."

"Ha, ha."

"Hey, you're the one who said you go there a lot."

"I meant, I go to—"

"Yeah, yeah. Change your story now." He smiled a bit, seemingly happy to be the one teasing me.

"Fine. You win," I said. I was rewarded with a full smile.

"What did you say?" His eyes twinkled.

"I said, you win. I don't really go there all the time. You caught me."

"Wow. I never thought I'd actually hear you say those words."

"That's because 90 percent of the time, I'm right. So enjoy it."

He folded another napkin. "Well, for your humbleness, I have a reward."

I grinned, "Tell me, tell me!"

"We got the ballistic report on the bullet."

"Really! What did they find?"

"They studied the riflings. It did come from a Winchester Special model 94. We checked with the county's gun registry, and Steve Miquel has a Winchester Special rifle registered to him. We're getting a search warrant for the rifle. He's under our microscope now, especially since his house is on the other side of the forest service land."

"You're kidding me. Are you saying Mr. Miquel shot at me? But why?"

"I'm not saying that, exactly. We don't have a motive. Like, nothing at all."

I rubbed my neck, feeling shook to the core. "That doesn't even make sense. I saw him leave before me that day."

"Did you actually see him leave?"

I frowned. "Well, I saw him with his car keys. He said he was his way to the golf course."

"Why would he be golfing when the ground's soggy and wet?"

That was true. I shrugged. "I have no idea."

"I can't wait to get my hands on that rifle."

"What do they check?"

"They'll be looking for striations on a fired bullet from his weapon to see if they match the bullet you recovered. They'll also be looking for firing-pin impressions to see if they're identical. But, in the meantime, they're still doing tests to see if there are any hidden fingerprints left on the bullet."

"Are you serious? A fingerprint? How is that even possible?"

"When the gun is loaded, it can leave a tiny bit of sweat from the fingertip. When the bullet is fired, the heat transfers the fingerprint by setting the salts into the metal."

"Wow, that's crazy."

He nodded.

"You slowpokes ready?" Cecelia appeared in the doorway, holding a casserole dish with a towel as a pot holder. "Can I get a hand here?"

I made a couple more trips for the water, napkins, and the other dish, while Cecelia called the guests to the dining room.

Lunch for us wasn't nearly so fancy—cold ham sandwiches eaten at the kitchen table. Frank left soon after we finished eating, but not before he gave me a hug.

"I thought you were grumpy with me," I said, snuggling into this shoulder.

"I'm always grumpy," he said, kissing the top of my head. I looked up at him and he bent down to kiss my lips.

"What's this?" Cecelia said, walking into the kitchen and catching us.

"Oh, you know," Frank said releasing me.

"I noticed you've been smiling more," she said. "Been good to see it."

He harrumphed. "She's already changing me," he said, before slamming the door.

Cecelia eyed the closed doorway before turning to me. "Good luck with that one."

"Thanks, I'm going to need it," I answered with a laugh. We started washing dishes, her washing and me drying.

"I have a question," I said, taking the pan from her hand. "Have you ever heard of GreenLeaf corporation?"

"Why are you asking?"

"I was trying to find out who owned a bar downtown. It said GreenLeaf did. But I thought that all the businesses were either independently owned, or leased by Marshall Incorporations. You know, Gayle and her husband's business?"

Cecelia handed me a plate. She sighed, which immediately perked my interest. Cecelia *did* know something!

"GreenLeaf is a secret," she finally admitted.

"Okay." I waited, my hand out for the next dish, nearly dancing in excitement.

She glanced at me and her lips puckered. "You aren't known for keeping secrets, GiGi."

My mouth dropped. "I certainly am!"

"No. No, you aren't. Remember that time I had that bike repainted for Frank, and you ran out to meet him, singing, 'What's red and blue and black all over?'"

I blushed. Grandma had brought me over to Cecelia's that day and I'd been fascinated watching the two women spray painting the bike the same colors as a bruise. I thought it would be a great joke to tease him. "To be fair, I was only about nine at the time."

Her near hairless eyebrows lifted. "Still..."

"Just tell me. Please." I made puppy dog eyes at her. Heck, if she was going to draw back on memories from over twenty years ago, so would I.

"GiGi Tanner, that will not work on me." She watched me for a second and then let out a deep breath. "Fine, but it goes no further than this room. GreenLeaf is a company that Gayle started for herself when their original company got into trouble for organizing a monopoly. It was a way to fly under the radar, so to speak. She slipped it out one night during Bingo. She was bragging about owning one of the state's last pay phones."

"During Bingo?" I was confused. That was a pretty big secret to let slip during such an innocuous game.

"Well, we *were* playing shot bingo." Cecelia laughed.

"You didn't!" I laughed.

"What? You think you young things have all the fun? We know how to whoop it up. Especially at Bingo." Her eyes twinkled.

Okay, then. That made me rethink all of her game nights. No wonder Cecelia was so eager to go.

I left that evening with my thoughts in a whirl. GreenLeaf belonged to Gayle Marshall. But what did that mean?

I felt like another visit to Gayle was in order.

CHAPTER 20

*I*t had been as simple as getting Gayle's phone number from Cecelia and then calling her. Cecelia had grumbled while giving me the number, but I told her I wasn't going to mention GreenLeaf, but rather a conversation that I'd overheard her having with Mrs. Vanderton on the night of the charity dinner.

Gayle Marshall had been pleasant on the phone, and invited me to stop by the next morning at around eleven. She sounded quite cooperative, affirming she'd be happy to speak with me. I may or may not have pretended I had the authority to ask her questions about Veronica Vanderton.

So, at eleven o'clock, I trotted up her walkway, noting the purple crocuses dotting along the bordering flowerbed. I couldn't help but smile as my eyes caught a few rebellious flowers poking their heads up randomly in the lawn. The gardener was going to have a field day when he saw those.

Gayle's house was a gorgeous manor built in the 1800s, and her porch was pristine on that cold morning, with the sunlight reflecting off of white railings and awning trim. I shifted a plate of muffins that I'd baked earlier to my other arm and firmly knocked.

As I waited, I glanced back behind me. A sluggish bee hovered over one of the first dandelions I'd seen this season before landing on the yellow bloom.

Firm footsteps came from inside the house and then the door opened. Gayle Marshall, wearing a silk eternity scarf and jacket, stood in the doorway.

"Hello," I said. "Did I catch you on your way out?"

"Hi there," she said. "No, I just felt like dressing up a bit today." She stepped back. "Come in."

I walked in as the sunshine flooded the entryway, washing out the paint color so it all appeared white. As she led me further into her house, I noticed it was a pale pink.

"So, what's that?" she asked, indicating the plate in my hand.

"Oh, these." I held them out. "I made some muffins. I hope you like them. I'm not a baking expert, but I was pretty pleased with this batch. Blueberry."

"How nice of you," she said, accepting them. She pulled back the wrapping and peeked inside. "They look delicious. Did you ever find out about the pin?"

She seemed so sincere. My doubts about her started to evaporate. So what if she owned the bar where the phone calls came from? Honestly, I was seeing suspects everywhere now.

"No, it's still a mystery," I admitted.

"The police actually came to see me." She raised her arm and I noticed a chunky bracelet on her arm. One in greens and purples, like the peacock pin. I swallowed hard.

"Oh, really?" I tried to act surprised.

"Yes. They found out that we'd made a bid on her house."

"Who's house? Mrs. Vanderton's?"

"Well, our corporation had. I suppose it will be the town gossip now."

"Did Mrs. Vanderton know?" I asked.

"It's possible. It was under..." here she hesitated. "Another offshoot of our division."

"Was it GreenLeaf?"

Her eyes sharpened like two points of obsidian as she stared at me. "How did you know?" The rich tone of her voice held a veiled threat.

Idiot! I yelled at myself. *Think fast.* "Uh, I thought I overheard it. Maybe at the grocery store?"

"What exactly did you hear?"

"Oh, just that the Marshall Corporation had branched out. That's very exciting. Good for you!" I gave her my brightest smile.

She studied me for a second and then seemed to soften. "Thank you. Not everyone understands. We're lucky to have such a successful company."

"It's quite an accomplishment," I agreed.

"So what was it you wanted to know?" She smiled, her friendly persona back in full force.

"I was curious about something I saw that night. I'd walked in on you two having a rather heated discussion."

"Oh, that poor woman." Gayle's forehead puckered as if in sorrow. "Unfortunately, she'd over heard a conversation Denise and I were having at the women's luncheon a couple weeks ago. It was about Veronica's foreclosure. Sadly, she didn't like what she heard."

I nodded. "I see, and I can imagine so." My mind was drawing a blank on the next thing to ask. "Well, that was really all I had. I'm sorry to have taken your time. I suppose I could have just asked over the phone. But then I would have missed an amazing chance to see your lovely home."

"Don't you love it?" She glanced around the giant entryway with a smile. "It truly is a dream come true. And no worries. I'm glad you stopped by. This way I get to try some of your yummy treats!" She lifted the plate in emphasis.

We said our goodbyes, and then I was back outside heading to my van.

As I shifted Old Bella into reverse to leave the driveway, I replayed the conversation. That actually went much better than I'd expected. Gayle hadn't thrown me out of her house, and she'd actually gave me quite a bit of information. I waved to the guard as I passed through the housing development's gate.

There *was* one thing that bothered me, though. What she had said about the house foreclosure rang true. From what I remembered, it really seemed to match Gayle's response to Veronica that night. I could actually picture the ladies luncheon and imagine Gayle and Denise Miquel chatting with catty laughter and being overheard by Veronica.

But there was one thing I had a problem with. When I'd

visited her antique store, Gayle had insisted she hadn't seen Veronica in nearly six months.

So, why would she say that? It didn't make sense that she'd say she hadn't seen her since last August, and then today tell me that the argument I'd overheard was from a meeting a few weeks before.

Gayle's lie, coupled with the fact that her company owned the Jack Knife where the three phone calls came from, had moved her higher on my list of suspects. I might not know her motive, but I was starting to see her fingerprints all over the place.

I was determined to figure out why.

CHAPTER 21

W hat could have motivated Gayle to kill Veronica? I literally twisted and turned in my bed for half the night, trying to figure out that puzzle. Gayle *had* to be guilty. It had to be her. She owned the bar where the phone calls came from. Sure, there was a phone booth, but the bartender also said there was an empty loft upstairs that the owners used. At the dinner, it was obvious the two women hated each other. And Gayle had lied about when she last saw Veronica. Plus, she'd admitted she was bidding on the widow's foreclosed house.

But what would make one rich person snap and kill another?

I took off my sleep mask and sat up in bed with a gasp. There was only one thing. One real thing.

Love.

Was the town forum gossip I read earlier about someone getting a "new nest with a married man" actually talking about Gayle? I remembered the bitter look on her face when she said that her husband wasn't her great love. It was a long shot, but Gayle had been the one to comfort Mr. Miquel the night of the charity dinner. And he'd called her love.

I bet Veronica found out about it. Maybe she was trying to extort them!

I jumped out of the covers and ran over to the computer. There had to be something, anything.

The first ten minutes of my online search was pretty bleak. It turned out it wasn't as simple as typing in the question, "Are Gayle Marshall and Steve Miguel having an affair?" That had to be it though. I remembered his ring finger, tan as the others as if he never wore a ring. My gut said that man was having an affair.

Finally, my persistence paid off.

It was on Gainesville's golfing board, of all places. Nothing much, but on the forum that was labeled "Weekly Gab" was this little tidbit from three weeks ago. "Top winner winning."

I clicked the topic and read the first post. "Hey Gainesville two-over-par. Better be more discreet on where you put your tee because momma's been hearing rumors."

I flipped back and read the tops scores for the week. Mr. Miquel was consistently a 108 putter.

I pushed back the laptop with a smile of satisfaction. This was it. I knew it. Proof he was having an affair.

I glanced at my phone. Two-thirty in the morning. Am I such a jerk that I'd message Frank right now with this news? No, I couldn't do it. I couldn't wake him up, knowing how hard it was for him to—

The phone buzzed in my hand. It was from Frank. That little stinker! Texting me at two-thirty in the morning? Trying to wake me up?

I opened it to read —**Listen. I know you're awake. We found the murder weapon. Want to talk?**

I wrote back —**Yes!**

The phone rang a millisecond after I pushed send. I answered it with an abrupt, "How the heck did you get that text so fast?"

"Huh? Oh I didn't. I just knew you'd say yes."

"And how would you know that?"

"Well, A. you're a night owl. And B. You're nosy."

I huffed into the phone, but knew he was right. "Well you got me up, so spill!"

"You weren't already awake?" He sounded unsure of himself.

I wanted to say no, but I knew it wouldn't be a clean win. I grudgingly admitted, "Yeah, I was."

He sighed in relief.

"But only because I figured out who the killer is!" I insisted, raising my trump card. "I was going to text you but I didn't want to wake you."

"Whatever. You should know by now I barely sleep," he said dismissively. "Anyway, who'd you come up with?"

"Gayle Marshall," I announced triumphantly.

"Really?" he asked, sounding surprised.

"Yes. She's the one who owns the building the phone calls came from. She was having an affair with Miguel."

"Well, who fired the rifle?"

I had an idea about that. "Her and her best friend used to be in competitive shooting in college. She has a ring from winning."

"This is sounding good. But how did she get Miquel's rifle? Assuming that's the one that was used."

"I guess I have to leave some of the detecting to you police guys."

He laughed. "Thanks so much. Anyway, you'll be happy to know the peacock pin we found was covered in toxin."

"Toxin?"

"It must have been soaking in that can of shrimp for a while. The coroner said a puncture from it was well enough to send someone into anaphylactic shock. And, interestingly enough, Veronica didn't have her EpiPen in her purse."

I gasped. "So Mr. Miquel must have taken it! He's in on it!"

"Now why do you think those two are having an affair?"

I told him about the Gainesville golf board, along with the gossip page I'd read earlier. And then I added, "It makes sense about the pin, because Gayle has a bunch of antique jewelry in her store."

"Mmm, this is good. But it's still conjecture. Don't you worry though, we're closing in on the murderer. Now get some sleep."

"Me? You get some sleep. And quit waking me."

He snorted a response, not taking me seriously. That's how you know someone really gets you.

I smiled and tried my best not to sound sappy. "Seriously, BigFoot, sleep well."

"You got it, Short Stuff."

I hung up the phone, knowing I looked like a sentimental idiot. But darn, that guy could be so cute. I had to laugh as I made my way back to the bed. We probably weren't the only couple in the world who teased each other in a show of affection.

I had to admit, I loved it.

THE NEXT DAY, while I was cleaning up from lunch at the B&B, Frank sent a text. **—Tracking down the tire tracks in the picture. Might be throwing a wrench in your theory.**

Wrench? What wrench? **—Don't ruin my plan. What is it?**

—Looks like the tracks come from a Mercedes-Benz. Just checked and Gayle drives a Range Rover.

My eyes popped open. I could feel my theory crumbling even as I tried to hang onto it.

189

I texted back—**So? It could have been someone else? Maybe a hunter.**

—Still investigating.

It's no big deal, I told myself, while gathering up the dishes. But in my heart, I just knew something was wrong. As perfect as this all was, something wasn't adding up.

There was just something I wasn't seeing.

I chucked the dish towel onto the counter. I wasn't going to give up. I just had to get more information on their affair. Someone out there had to have seen something. But who would give me the scoop?

"What's up, GiGi? Why the long face?" Cecelia said. I hadn't heard her enter the kitchen.

I blew out a big breath. "I have this feeling Miquel is having an affair with Gayle. I found some confirmation on a couple internet pages. Have you ever been to the Gainesville golf club?"

"Of course. I was a member there at one time."

"Really?"

"Yes, but I let the membership go when my husband died. It was really for him after all. Quite the catty place. The Miquel's are members there. And of course the Marshall's."

She thought for a moment. "And Veronica Vanderton as well, now that I think of it."

I nodded. "Speaking of catty, any guesses on who would have left a catty remark on the forum about a married man having an affair?"

"Oh, those are anonymous, right?"

"They can be. People make up names for themselves."

She pursed her lips, thinking. "Then it could have been anyone. People like to spill scandals around here."

"What do you think? Was Steve Miquel capable of an affair? How was their marriage?"

"I definitely think he's capable of it." Cecelia frowned as she got a mug down from the cupboard. She filled it with coffee and continued. "The thing is, Denise and Gayle go way back. They were best friends before either of them married. They went to college and did many competitive tournaments together. I have a hard time seeing Gayle betray her friend like that."

I groaned. Another coffin nail to my theory besides the tire prints. "But it could happen, right? People do scummy things like betray friends."

She nodded and blew on her coffee. "That's true. However, those types of things are rare in a friendship like that. I'd more likely believe that Denise would off her husband and go live with Gayle, then Gayle cheat with Steve Miquel."

I bit the inside of my cheek in frustration. "Is there anything else you might have forgotten at the Miguel house?"

She narrowed her eyes at me. "What are you thinking, GiGi?"

I shrugged and tried to look innocent. "Nothing much. I just thought maybe I could have a conversation with their housekeeper. We kind of hit it off the last time."

She sighed and shook her head. "Girl, you've always kept me and your grandma hopping. Alway a handful, you were."

I glanced around the kitchen. "I mean, you might have left a potholder, right?"

She snorted. "As a matter of fact, I do think I left a crystal carafe there. Either that, or maybe Adele snagged it. Why don't you go track that down?"

Yes! "You've got it." I jumped up and headed for the hall.

"Oh? Leaving right now?" she asked with a smirk.

I skidded to a stop. "Do you need me? I'm sorry. I didn't ask."

She laughed and shooed me with her hand. "Get out of here."

I jumped into the van and chucked the phone into the cup

holder before buckling my seatbelt. Just before I shifted into drive, the phone dinged with an incoming message from Frank. —**Miquel's alibi turned out to be good. He was at the golf course. But the rifle is turning out to be a dead end. Miguel says it's been stolen.**

Stolen? Cold chills ran up my spine. The sun was shining, the grass was green. I was on my way to learn more about the affair. It should be a great day.

But instead, I felt like my carefully constructed house of cards was falling apart. Was there going to be an easy answer to any of this?

Fifteen minutes later, I turned into the Miquel's driveway and started to pull around to the side. A car had followed after me. I parked and watched it in my rearview mirror.

My jaw dropped.

It was a Mercedes-Benz.

CHAPTER 22

I sat frozen, my eyes glued to my rearview mirror.

The car door opened and a woman wearing heels glided out. Glamour should have been her middle name. She wore dark glasses, and a fitted dress suit, and her blonde hair was teased and sprayed into the type of updo that would rival the ones on the red carpet. She glanced in my direction and seemed to dismiss me, probably taking Old Bella for a delivery van. She strolled into the house, self-possessed and confident.

I noted that she hadn't knocked. This must be the mysterious Mrs. Denise Miquel. It sure seemed bizarre that Steve would cheat on her.

I exhaled a breath that I hadn't realized I'd been holding and climbed out of the van. Compared to the way Mrs. Miquel moved, I felt like a stray dog as I scurried to the servant's entrance.

The housekeeper answered the door. "Georgie! How are you! What brings you here?"

My mind was spinning after seeing whom I presumed was Mrs. Miquel, especially in *that* car. *Pull it together.* "Uh, Cecelia was thinking she may have left her crystal carafe here. I was in the neighborhood, and just thought I'd stop to check." I inwardly cringed. In the neighborhood? Yeah, like I normally mosey around a million-dollar neighborhood. Seeing that Mercedes-Benz had really thrown me off my game.

"Oh, well come in. Let's go check."

She led me down the hallway that I was growing so familiar with, and we entered the kitchen. The housekeeper murmured the question and the cook pointed to where she kept her carafes. We walked to the butler's pantry and examined them. I had no idea what Cecelia's looked like, but the housekeeper apparently found one that was unfamiliar and plucked it out.

"Why don't you ask Cecelia if this is hers?" she said, handing it over to me.

I grabbed hold of it, thinking it might look familiar after all.

After a quick glance at the cook pottering about washing dishes, I decided to be bold.

"I don't want to put you in an awkward place but..."—here I lowered my voice while she leaned in closer.

Eagerness widened her eyes. "Yes?"

"I heard a rumor," I whispered darkly. "It involves Mr. Miquel."

Her mouth rounded to a silent O. She backed away and nodded sagely. "I'm sure you have."

"So, is it true?" I could hardly keep the excitement from trilling through my voice. "Is he having an affair?"

The housekeeper made the same backwards glance toward the cook. Seeing that she was still distracted with the dishes, the housekeeper turned back to me. "Well, it's not my place to say, but he's rarely at home. And when he returns, he smells of violets." Her eyebrow lifted as if I should know what that meant.

"Does her husband know?" I asked.

The housekeeper's brows lowered in question. "Husband?"

"Ms. Kimber!" A razor-edged voice snapped behind us. I confess, we both jumped and looked guiltily in that direction.

"Ma'am," The housekeeper glanced to the floor.

Mrs. Miquel stood there. Her elegant face wore an expression so sharp it could have cut brie. I felt the blood drain from my face. How long had she been standing there? What had she heard?

"Can I ask what you are doing?" Mrs. Miquel's gaze sliced between me and Ms. Kimber.

"Ma'am. She's here to pick up a decanter. It was left the night of the dinner."

I held up the referred to crystal for Mrs. Miquel's approval.

Mrs. Miquel ignored the item. "Well, it seems to be found. Shall we continue with our day, then?"

"Yes, ma'am." Ms. Kimber left. I could almost feel her relief as she disappeared around the corner.

Mrs. Miquel watched the housekeeper go, and then flashed me a frosty smile. "All set, then?"

I swallowed hard. "Y-yes. Just needed this. I guess I'll be on my way."

I smiled and sidled past her. The cook was still washing dishes, seemingly oblivious to the interaction that had happened behind her. My heart pounded as I reached the back door and it was all I could do not to run to my van and make my escape.

All that was spinning through my mind was, "She heard! She heard!" I wanted to scream.

I drove to the bed-and-breakfast and presented the carafe to Cecelia. She claimed it with a laugh, saying that it was, indeed, the missing one.

"And how about you, GiGi?" Cecelia asked. "Did you find anything you were looking for?"

I nodded woodenly. "But I'm more confused than ever."

She studied my face before clucking her tongue. Quickly, she made me a cup of tea and pressed a cookie into my hand. "Take this and go on outside. It's surprising how restorative the power of the outdoors is to my clear thinking. I bet it will help."

I gave her a hug as a thank you, and took my snack outside. The sunshine warmed my face as I sat on the porch steps and leaned against the railing. I stared into the back yard.

The maple trees had tight leaf buds on all their branches. Cecelia had done a beautiful job with cleaning and pruning the rose garden, and now all that remained was to remove the mulch around the roots in the next few weeks. It was a lovely piece of property, but it sure took a lot of work for its upkeep.

A flutter caught my attention. There, hopping in front of me was a robin. It tilted its head and watched me with one of its beady black eyes.

Little red breast, one of my favorite things about spring. A true sign that winter was at its end.

"Hi, sweet thing. You going to catch a worm?" I whispered at it. Carefully, I broke off a crumb from my cookie and tossed it in the bird's direction.

The bird hopped a few feet, still staring at me. It pecked at the cookie crumb, then took to wing and flew away.

I watched it go, still trying to figure everything out.

Think, Georgie, think. The Mercedes Benz was being driven by Denise Miquel. Was it the rental Mr. Miquel mentioned in the phone call? She wasn't at the charity dinner. Ms. Kimber seemed to validate that Mr. Miquel was having an affair. Was it possible that Denise Miquel could have committed murder? But why Veronica? And what was Ms. Kimber was going to say when I asked about Gayle's husband?

Mrs. Miquel dressed and acted so sophisticated that it was hard to picture her committing murder. But maybe if she had a strong enough motive.

I took a sip of my tea. Suddenly, I started choking as it went down the wrong pipe. The motive had hit me like a leaden ball.

How could I have been so dumb?

CHAPTER 23

*A*s soon as I recovered, I ran inside the B&B and grabbed a notepad and pen from the desk in the study.

"You okay, GiGi?" Cecelia called as I rushed by the kitchen on my way back outside.

"Yep, just getting things down."

I sat on the porch steps and started to make a list of questions.

1. Why were tire tracks matching Denise Miquel's car description on the side of the logging road?
2. Why did both Denise Miguel and Gayle Marshall hate Veronica Vanderton?

3. WHERE WAS the rifle now? Has it really been stolen?

4. Who made the phone calls and shot at me?

I READ my list over and then texted Frank. —**Is there any way Denise Miquel's alibi can be checked on the night of the dinner?**

His response was immediate. —**Is there a way? That's like asking if the sky is blue. I'll have it in an hour.**

I smiled as I read it. He didn't even ask me why, like he knew I wouldn't ask without a good reason. *That guy really gets me.*

Still, I thought I'd let him in. —**She drives a Mercedes Benz.**

He wrote back. —**Close. We've already checked that. She actually drives a Bentley.**

I typed back— **I saw her exit a Mercedes Benz at her house. I overheard Mr. Miquel's phone conversation that night yelling at someone. A car rental was mentioned. Maybe it was her rental?**

Lots of dots showed he was typing, but his answer was short and dissatisfying.—**That's quite a discovery.**

I was thinking about something witty to say in response, when he wrote again. —**Listen Inspector Gadget, stay out of trouble. We've got this.**

I harrumphed and slid the phone away. I didn't want him mad at me again. Of course I'd take his advice.

Sort of.

I drained the last bit of my tea and walked back into the house.

"Feeling better, GiGi?" Cecelia asked, looking up from where she was mixing something that smelled chocolatey and delicious in a bowl.

"I think so." I spotted the cookie jar, and bet Cecelia had just loaded it up. I considered it for a minute. Well, food always did have a way of greasing stubborn doors.

"Would you be opposed to me taking a plate of cookies? I'd like to bring something to Veronica Vanderton's sister as a way of showing our condolences."

"Of course, dear. I'm always happy to show condolences." Her voice was sweet but her eyes narrowed as she watched me. Still, she didn't question my motives. I grabbed a plastic plate from the pantry and loaded it up, before covering it with plastic wrap.

"You okay with me leaving again?" I asked.

"We should be fine until dinner time," she answered, retrieving a bundt pan from a lower cupboard.

"All right. I'll see you later."

I was gambling that I knew where the sister was staying. I figured she'd be at Veronica's house. After a quick search, I was on my way.

I pulled into the colonial home's driveway—most likely built in the 1770s. She lived in a very old neighborhood, the road bordered by stately maple trees. There was a small compact car in the driveway with plates that marked it as a rental.

I pulled past the driveway and parked Old Bella out on the street, feeling like the vehicle stood out like a sore thumb. I didn't even lock it when I got out. Let's face it, anyone who rifled through the van in search for something to steal would sadly be disappointed. They'd only leave with a candy bar wrapper and a proof of insurance.

Anxiety was ticking around at the base of my throat. I never considered myself an introvert, more like a non-talking extrovert. I liked being in the world and around people. Just don't approach to me.

So knocking on a stranger's door was, once again, going against my core of what felt comfortable. But I was curious and determined, and those forces were an automatic override of anything else.

Armed with my plate of cookies, I marched up the sidewalk. I found if I didn't give myself time to think, things went easier.

Azalea bushes lined the walkway up to the front porch. I trotted up the stairs and knocked on the door. Feeling slightly shaky, I stood back and waited.

The door opened, and a woman in her forties stood there. She was dressed nicely, and appeared to come from money, but other than that, she seemed to have little in common with her sister.

"Hello," I said. "I'm Georgie Tanner. My friend is one of the officers investigating what happened to Veronica Vanderton. He told me her sister was in town. I just wanted to stop by to offer my condolences."

"Oh." Her expression softened and her gaze dropped down to the plate in my hands.

"For you," I said, lifting it up.

"Oh, well thank you." She accepted the plate and stood back from the doorway. "I'm Amelia Spalding, Veronica's sister. Won't you come in?"

I followed her into the house, my head swiveling around as I tried to take everything in. What hit me first was the overload of paintings on the wall and knick-knacks galore lit by a sparkling chandelier overhead.

And the scent of violets.

"The living room is this way," she said, leading me in deeper through the old home.

She took me in to what Cecelia would term the parlor, and we sat opposite each other on stiff, ugly loveseats.

"I so appreciate you stopping by. I'm just trying to get through Veronica's things. I'm the executer."

"I'm so sorry. Do you need help?" I asked.

"Well, I'm having an estate sale soon. This place will be out of my hands. You see, she was—" Mrs. Spalding stuttered and blushed. "She was in default on her loan. It's being reverted back to the bank."

"I'm so sorry." I cleared my throat. "I *had* heard rumors of a short sale."

She nodded. "Yes, Veronica was doing everything possible to escape that. The last time I'd talked to her, she said she had a plan. She was positive she would come up with the money in time."

"Oh, you'd heard from her recently?" That went against the information Frank had given me, that they hadn't been speaking for several years.

"Yes. It was kind of out of the blue. We hadn't talked for quite some time. You see, she was having an affair. Frankly, we disapproved. It led to an ugly falling out that neither of us seemed to be able to bridge. And then one day, she calls. Naturally, the fact that she wanted financial help didn't please my husband. Unfortunately, with today's economy we weren't in a position to do much." Mrs. Spalding made a helpless motion with her hands.

"I completely understand." I nodded.

"Then, Veronica called me back a few weeks ago and told me not to worry. That she had everything figured out. I asked her how, and she said she had some good news, that she was breaking off the affair, and that someone would be giving her a check at the charity dinner she'd be attending soon. She actually sounded hopeful. It was such a different tone then I was used to hearing from her. She was usually so"—Mrs. Spalding seemed to be searching for a word —"condescending."

I took a deep breath and bobbed my head again. Time for the big guns. I clenched my hand to strengthen my courage. "Do you know who Veronica was having an affair with?"

She glanced at me in surprise. "What? I thought everyone knew. I figured that's why she was so disliked in this town."

"Disliked?" I licked my lips that had gone paper-dry.

"I thought you knew. She died at his house, you know."

My blood ran cold. From this morning, I had suspected, but I honestly was still shocked at having it confirmed. Veronica Vanderton and Mr. Miquel. Of course. I remembered the way he touched her cheek at the dinner, and how, after she'd died, he'd said he'd lost everything. At the time, I thought he was feeling passionate about the loss of his sword. But now it all made sense.

But I still didn't know who killed Veronica. Was it Mrs. Miquel? She had the strongest motive. What was this about Veronica getting money to cover her defaulted loan? And who stole the sword?

The questions whirled in my mind. We chatted for a few more minutes, with our conversation ending with me again extending my condolences. I tried to leave her my phone number in case she should need help in some way, but she assured me that her brother was flying in that week.

Back out on the sidewalk, I tried to digest everything I knew. My thoughts were thick and spinning, and I wanted to get hold of Frank right away.

I stepped out onto the sidewalk, still deep in thought. A dog barking snapped me out of my reverie and I looked up.

There was a car hurtling straight at me.

CHAPTER 24

The driver in the car twisted the wheel and the car jumped onto the sidewalk. I dove toward the grass and landed on my side. The fall knocked the air out of me. I felt a gust as the car's tires passed within inches of my feet.

The driver spun the wheel, and the car's tires chewed up the dirt as it flew back to the road, narrowing avoiding impact with one of the maple trees.

I lay there with my mouth gaping like a fish, struggling to breathe. *Have to. Move. Have to. Move.* I rolled to my side and tried to crawl toward the porch.

Squealing tires signaled the car disappearing around the corner. I heard its engine revving as it sped away.

"Good heavens! Are you okay?" Mrs. Spalding crouched next to me. I hadn't heard the front door open.

I couldn't nod. I struggled to breathe. *Relax, this will pass.* Like a syphon, suddenly I was able to suck in a breath. Greedily I gasped, arms splayed out on the grass.

"Oh, honey," Mrs. Spalding fretted, two wrinkles deepening between her eyebrows.

I glanced in her direction, still gasping in relief. But I nodded and gave her a thumbs up to alleviate her worry.

She patted my arm. "Is there anything I can do to help?"

Slowly, I shook my head and then rolled to my side. I sat up, still sucking in air. My ribs ached, and each breath felt like fire.

The effects of the adrenaline kicked in then, and my body started to tremble. *Somebody just tried to run me over!* I plucked my phone out of my pocket, hoping I hadn't crushed it.

It was fine, but a bruise on my hip from where I'd landed on it made me yelp when I drew my phone out. I dialed Frank. No time for texting now.

"How ya doing, Short Stuff?" he answered, sounding somewhat cheerful.

I cringed, knowing I was about to ruin it. "Uh, Frank...."

"What's wrong?" Immediately his voice became tight.

I swallowed. "Someone just tried to run me over."

"What? Where are you?"

I grimaced as I sat up straighter. Grass and leaves stuck in my hair. I started to pluck them out. "Outside Veronica Vanderton's place."

"What kind of car? Describe everything you remember." His voice was pure business.

"Yellow. Two door. Small. A spoiler on the back. Last three digits of the license plate are D44"

"Got it," he said. "Don't move, I'm sending help."

I hung up and looked at Mrs. Spalding gratefully. "Thank you so much. I'm sure it's because he saw you that he left. Help is on its way."

"I saw the car too," she said. "I can describe it to them if you want."

It was about five minutes before I heard sirens. Officer Jefferson was the cop who showed up. He took our statements, but before he finished, he had a call on his mic. He listened and then keyed back, "ten-four."

He had a big smile as he faced us. "They caught him."

"Really? That fast?" I said.

"Yeah, we had him pulled over just a few nights ago, so we had an idea of who he was and where he was heading. They caught him with dirt and grass still crammed into his fender.

I laid back in the grass in relief. And then I told Jefferson, "Send someone to Miquel's house. Denise Miquel might be trying to make her escape."

I'd forgotten I wasn't talking to Frank. Officer Jefferson smiled at me in the most pacifying way. "You just rest. You've had a lot of stress this morning."

Frustrated, I pulled out my phone and sent a text to Frank. — **Please, go to Miquel's house. She's the one who killed Veronica Vanderton.**

My phone rang.

"Give me something," Frank said. His voice was still stiff and unemotional. I could imagine his colleagues were with him.

"Denise killed Veronica." I heard a gasp and realized Mrs. Spalding was still standing next to me. But it couldn't be helped. I needed to make sure they caught Denise before she left.

"She never went to her mother's, or at least she went later

212

than she said. Miguel and Veronica were having an affair. Veronica went to Denise to make a deal, probably in exchange for leaving her husband alone. Veronica was desperate to save her house from being sold to her arch enemy, Gayle. Denise made a plan to meet Veronica in the study during dinner to give her the money. Instead, Denise stabbed her with the tainted pin."

"We're already on our way to pick her up. Her alibi timeline was off by four hours from when she'd said she'd been with her mother. There are some pieces missing, but we had enough to bring her in for questioning." He cleared his throat. "You done giving a statement?"

"Yeah," I said. "Mrs. Spalding saw the car, so she collaborated the color and style."

"Oh, I don't think we're going to have any trouble with this guy. He's singing in tune with the color of his car. Just like a canary."

"Who was it?" I asked, hesitant to find out.

"Robert the valet from the other night. And let me tell you, he's got a story to tell." His voice softened. "Go back to the B&B so I don't worry about you. I'll stop by when I'm done."

I wanted to reassure him not to worry about me, but my ribs hurt too badly for that. Instead, I found myself more than willing to agree.

Officer Jefferson helped me to my feet, and I limped over to my van. Apparently, I'd twisted my ankle in my dive for safety.

"Excuse me, Georgie?" Mrs. Spalding's anxious face appeared at my opened van door. I cringed, remembering what she'd overheard.

"I'm so sorry," I said, shaking my head. "I'm so, so sorry. I never meant for you to hear that." I couldn't imagine what the poor woman was going through.

"No, it's all right. I mean, it's not all right, but I'm glad I know." She breathed heavily, her narrow nose flaring. "You know, it's ironic. I always warned Veronica. I told her she was playing with fire. I just had a feeling something like this would happen."

I nodded, not knowing what to say.

Her bottom lip trembled, and I reached out a hand to pat her arm. Ever so slightly, she pulled away, and straightened her spine, composing herself. "You lay with dogs, you're bound to pick up fleas." She gave an emphatic nod.

"They're not going to get away with it. Justice will be done." I said.

"Justice?" She turned and eyed the house, and then crossed her arms over her chest. "Justice has never brought someone back. Veronica made her choices. Nothing I said could ever make her see that she was going the wrong way." And without another word, Mrs. Spalding walked up the driveway and entered the house.

I felt sick. I really did. The world could get so dark and dirty. Sometimes, it was hard to see the light.

My ribs throbbed, reminding me that I needed to get to the B&B. Heaven help me if Frank arrived there before I did.

I started the van and drove to Baker street, feeling emptier than I had in a long, long time.

CHAPTER 25

Frank had filled Cecilia in, and she'd pampered me and fussed over me from the moment I pulled into the driveway. Soon after I walked into the house, she had me settled in the living room in front of the fire with a quilt drawn up over my lap. Soft music played in the background. I leaned my head back against the chair and closed my eyes, loving the down time.

The valet had tried to run me over. Crazy. But it made me remember how I'd caught him talking angrily into his phone that night. I wondered now at what his involvement was. I couldn't wait to talk to Frank.

It turned out it was going to be a while before he came over. But he'd promised to call me from the station, after they finished the interview with Robert Evans.

CRÈME BRÛLÉE TO SLAY

After an hour of relaxation, I decided I needed some fresh air. Maybe I could take Bear for a walk. I poked my head into the kitchen to let Cecelia know. She wasn't happy with me leaving.

"Frank told me to keep my eye on you!" But having just ascribed to the medical restorative powers of fresh air not more than a couple hours earlier, she probably felt she couldn't say no. With a swoosh of the dish towel in my direction, she shooed me out.

I walked over to Oscar's place, hoping he wouldn't be too put out if I just showed up. He was a stickler for a schedule, that one.

He answered the door with his usual gruff frown, his hair sticking up in the back.

"Did I wake you?" I asked.

"What? No. I never nap." He followed my gaze to the hair tufts on top his head, and sent an arthritic hand up to go smooth them down. "Just checking my eyelids for pinholes is all."

That caused a chuckle to come out of me, followed by a groan as the pain in my ribs flared.

"You okay?" His eyes flicked to where my hand clutched my side.

"I'm fine. Just almost got run over by a car. Hurt my ribs diving to safety."

"Mm," he said noncommittally, but his eyes sparkled with a bit of respect.

"Remind you of your FBI days?" I asked, hinting. I really wanted to ask him why Derek's name had caused such a reaction. Maybe Oscar had chased someone with the same last name at one point?

"You liked that tidbit, did you?" He smiled and rubbed his white whiskered chin, obviously pleased with himself that he'd been able to surprise me. Then, his eyes narrowed. "Now, why are you here?" Back to gruff as usual.

"I was wondering if I could walk Bear," I said, waggling my fingers at the Pomeranian who jumped up against my leg at the sound of my voice.

"Walk her? Confounded thing does anything but walk. She flies, jumps, rolls, twists, and gets stuck. Wish the little fluff ball would walk." His smile betrayed his complaining as he glanced at the dog.

I started to chuckle again, but quickly cut it off.

He noticed my grimace. "And you, Missy, are in no shape to tackle a monster like her. She'd tear you apart and leave you for dead."

The monster in question smiled up at me, her pink tongue panting. "I very much doubt that, Oscar." Slowly I eased myself to sitting on his top step. The wood creaked under my weight, reminding me of how Frank and I were soon going to replace the treads. Bear set her two front feet on my leg and licked my cheek. Then, she sprang down the stairs, yipping wildly. I looked to see what she was chasing.

Another robin, which quickly flew up into the tree.

Robin, my sign of spring. My sign of hope.

As if sensing what I was thinking, Oscar muttered, "Trees are like people, you know that? Some trees bring shelter to helpless creatures. Some bring shade, some food. But it's only the strong ones that can weather the storms. Their roots grow deeper and their branches wider. They grow stronger. And they are able to give even more."

His words brought tears to my eyes. I knew he'd weathered some storms, and he knew some of mine. We sat there in silence. After a moment, he whistled through his teeth. "Bear! Come here, Bear."

The little Pomeranian ignored him.

"Bear!" He snapped his fingers.

The dog turned and panted, pink tongue lolling out.

"Come here you little fuzz ball," he growled.

CEECEE JAMES

The dog's dark eyes watched him as if deciding if her owner was serious, before a grasshopper caught her interest. She immediately sprang after it.

"Confound it. Peanut! Come here."

The dog abandoned the insect and came bounding over toward Oscar. She scampered up the stairs, her nails scrabbling against the wood. He caught her in his arms with a wheezy grunt and lifted her to his chest. Mumbling words I couldn't understand, he returned into the house, shutting the door behind him.

Well, okay then. I guess the conversation was over. I smiled, despite myself, wondering what else I was going to do until Frank called.

My phone rang. Easing to my side ever so carefully, I gently slid it out.

"Hello?" I gasped.

"Georgie? Are you okay?" Frank's voice was full of concern.

"I'm fine. Just a little bruised. Tell me how the meeting went!"

"Well, this will be Robert Evans' third strike. He was ready to make a deal."

"Oh, great!"

"You were right. Denise Miquel did murder Veronica Vanderton for having an affair with her husband. And, you were right, Veronica did try to extort money from Denise to pay off her house loan."

I leaned against the stair tread. I'd been right. I knew it. "I remember him crying when she died. He touched her cheek. He looked so lost and devastated. He didn't know Denise's plan, did he?"

"We brought Steve Miquel in too, and he fully cooperated. He says he expected his wife at the dinner, and had been blindsided when Denise said she was with her sick mother."

I nodded. That must have been the phone call I'd overheard when he was in the foyer. "What was Robert's role? Was Gayle guilty?"

"Robert got roped into it because Denise gave him the bail money for his drug trafficking charge."

I remembered Frank mentioning the charge when they pulled the valet over the other night.

"Okay," I said, nodding. "But how on earth did Denise get connected with him in the first place?"

"The Marshall's Bickford Enterprises shipping company was used for the drug smuggling crime that Robert got arrested for. Of course, Gayle came to Denise to commiserate when it happened. Denise kept the information in her back pocket. She'd been planning this for a while, and knew she'd need someone willing to commit a crime. At some point, she searched who'd been arrested and approached Robert, offering him money for a lawyer in exchange for help. "

"Got it."

"So Robert described the charity night like this. Supposedly, he didn't know that Veronica was going to be murdered. His role was supposed to be simple. Denise needed him to keep a look out, and to later sell the sword. After Denise stabbed Veronica with the pin, she went into the conference room and swiped the war relic. She must have dropped the peacock pin there on accident when she picked the sword up. Her motive for stealing the sword was to muddy the waters, hoping to get the police interested in the stolen party, rather than dig too deeply into how Veronica had died."

After that, Denise snuck out the back door and slipped through the forest service land, maybe using the same app you did, to where she'd left her rental car. From there, she'd simply taken off and driven to her mother's. Which was why her time line was four hours off from what she's given to the police."

"Got it," I said, following.

"Robert was supposed to fence the sword for her. When we

caught him the other night, he'd just dropped it off at that house that sells stolen goods."

"Wow. Can you track it?" I asked.

"Detective Kirby is on it. The fencers are being surprisingly cooperative in the face of the threat of having their computer records being torn apart."

"That's good news. By the way, I know who shot at me."

"Are you going to say Gayle Marshall?" Frank asked.

"I thought it was her for a hot minute, but then realized it couldn't have been. It was Denise. See, I'd been so focused on Gayle, that I'd forgotten that Denise had also been in all those sharp-shooting competitions. She was an expert shot. But what really sealed it for me was the fact that only Denise or Miquel had access to their gun safe where the Winchester was kept. It just made sense.""

"Well, you're right. Robert said that after Denise had been questioned by the cookies, and then finding out that Robert had nearly been caught with the sword, she freaked out. Apparently, she saw you eyeing the woods behind their house, and then your phone, and she got suspicious. She followed you out the back door and waited in the woods on a hunch that you might show up. And you did. She wanted to scare you off from snooping."

"I was *right*." I was proud of myself.

"What a fun thing to be right about," Frank said sarcastically.

"What? I like figuring these things out. I've been putting the pieces together for a while, but at Veronica Vanderton's house I realized that only Denise had a real motive for murder. And she had access to the peacock pin, being that Gayle was her best friend and owned the antique shop."

"So you think Gayle is still guilty somehow then?" Frank asked.

I shook my head, even though he couldn't see. "No. Gayle *did* know about the affair though. I remember the Johnsons remarking about how Gayle poked Veronica all throughout the charity dinner. I also overheard Gayle cut off some gossip at the table about Valerie being with a married man. She didn't want her best friend exposed." I sighed. "I just wish we knew where the rifle was."

"Well, I'm a gift that keeps on giving," Frank answered. "You remember how Miquel claimed it was stolen? Maybe he really thought it was, I don't know. It's just too bad for them that we found the Winchester Special model 94 rifle in the trunk of Denise's rental car. I'm sure she meant to dispose of it. Forensics is working on it right now."

"Yes!" I yelled it out, and then winced and curled over. Softer, I asked, "So I'm guessing Denise made the phone calls to scare me?"

"Yep. Made from the pay phone. Denise hoped that by doing them from a seedy place like that, it would throw everyone off her trail even more. She knew about the place since Gayle had bragged about the phone a few times."

"It's all just so crazy." I said. I really didn't know what else to say. People did terrible things for love or revenge. I couldn't help to think what a horrible person Denise Miquel was. *But what if the man I loved was cheating on me?* Spurned love and betrayal could do strange things to the human mind.

Frank cleared his throat. "Err, one last thing. Sheriff Parker was asking how you got wrapped up in this. I told him you were nosy, and he said he's hoping that you'll be staying out of our town's next murder."

I laughed and moaned.

"Aww, you hurting that much?"

"Only when I breathe," I admitted.

"That's too bad. I was planning on taking you for a picnic this weekend. Down by McAllister's farm. Remember that place?" I could hear the smile in his voice.

"I sure do." I could really use a break. Just thinking about a fun afternoon away made my muscles relax. I clutched the phone tighter to my ear. "Remember chasing each other in that corn field?"

"I seem to remember you chasing me." He teased. I could tell he thought that I'd been chasing him all along because he was hot stuff.

"Well, buddy," I grinned. "I can confess it now. It was the best trick I had. Having you run before me swept all those spider webs away."

He chuckled, making those butterflies go crazy in my stomach. His voice was warm like caramel when he finally answered. "You don't think I didn't know that? Baby girl, I got you. I'll alway be there to knock those spider webs down for you."

Tears stung my eyes. "I don't say it enough, Frank. You are one in a million. I've got you, too."

The End

Thank you for reading Crème Brûlée To Slay. Book four, Drizzle of Death, will be out soon! Here are two more mystery series to whet your appetite in the meantime. All are free with Kindle Unlimited.

Oceanside Hotel Cozy Mysteries

Booked For Murder

Deadly Reservation

Final Check Out

Fatal Vacancy

Angel Lake Cozy Mysteries

The Sweet Taste of Murder

The Bitter Taste of Betrayal

The Sour Taste of Suspicion

The Honeyed Taste of Deception

The Tempting Taste of Danger

The Frosty Taste of Scandal

Made in the USA
Middletown, DE
23 November 2018